FIRST STORY

First Story changes lives through writing.

We believe that writing can transform lives, and that there is dignity and power in every young person's story.

First Story brings talented, professional writers into secondary schools serving low-income communities to work with teachers and students to foster creativity and communication skills. By helping students find their voices through intensive, fun programmes, First Story raises aspirations and gives students the skills and confidence to achieve them.

For more information and details of how to support First Story, see www.firststory.org.uk or contact us at info@firststory.org.uk.

The Multiverses
ISBN 978-0-85748-303-4

Published by First Story Limited
www.firststory.org.uk
Omnibus Business Centre,
39–41 North Road
London
N7 9DP

Typesetting: Avon DataSet Ltd
Cover Designer: Francesca Winterman
Printed in the UK by Aquatint

The Multiverses

An Anthology

BY THE FIRST STORY GROUP
AT THE FARNBOROUGH ACADEMY

EDITED AND INTRODUCED BY PAULA RAWSTHORNE | 2018

FIRST STORY

Changing lives through writing

'We all have a voice. Some never discover it. We all have stories to tell. Some never tell them. First Story has helped all these young writers to discover their writing voice, and in so doing has helped them discover themselves.'

Michael Morpurgo (author of *War Horse*)

'First Story is a fantastic idea. Creative writing can change people's lives: I've seen it happen. It's more than learning a skill. It's about learning that you, your family, your culture and your view of the world are rich and interesting and important, whoever you happen to be. Teenagers are under increasing pressure to tailor their work to exams, and to value themselves in terms of the results. First Story offers young people something else, a chance to find their voices.'

Mark Haddon (author of *The Curious Incident of the Dog in the Night-Time*)

'First Story not only does an invaluable thing for the young and under-heard people of England, it does it exceptionally well. Their books are expertly edited and beautifully produced. The students featured within are wonderfully open and candid about their lives, and this is a credit to First Story, whose teachers thoroughly respect, and profoundly amplify, their voices. The only problem with First Story is that they're not everywhere – yet. Every young person deserves the benefit of working with them.'

Dave Eggers (author of *A Heartbreaking Work of Staggering Genius*)

'First Story is an inspiring initiative. Having attended a school with a lot of talented kids who didn't always have the opportunity to express that talent, I know what it would have meant to us to have real-life writers dropping by and taking our stories seriously. And what an opportunity for writers, too, to meet some of the most creative and enthusiastic young people in this country! It's a joyful project that deserves as much support as we can give it.'

Zadie Smith (winner of the Orange Prize for fiction and author of *White Teeth*)

As Patron of First Story I am delighted that it continues to foster and inspire the creativity and talent of young people in secondary schools serving low-income communities.

I firmly believe that nurturing a passion for reading and writing is vital to the health of our country. I am therefore greatly encouraged to know that young people in this school – and across the country – have been meeting each week throughout the year in order to write together.

I send my warmest congratulations to everybody who is published in this anthology.

Camilla

HRH The Duchess of Cornwall

Thank You

Kate Kunac-Tabinor, **Lucy Cowdery**, **Chris Scotcher**, and all the designers at **OUP** for their overwhelming support for First Story, and **Francesca Winterman** specifically, for giving their time to design this anthology.

Melanie Curtis at **Avon DataSet** for her overwhelming support for First Story and for giving her time in typesetting this anthology.

Nishul Shah for copy-editing this anthology and supporting the project.

Moya Birchall at **Aquatint** for printing this anthology at a discounted rate.

Open Gate Trust for supporting First Story in this school.

HRH The Duchess of Cornwall, Patron of First Story.

The Trustees of First Story:
Andrea Minton Beddoes, Antonia Byatt, Aslan Byrne, Beth Colocci, Betsy Tobin, Charlie Booth, Edward Baden-Powell, James Waldegrave, Katie Waldegrave, Mayowa Sofekun, Sophie Harrison, Sue Horner, William Fiennes.

The Advisory Board of First Story:
Alex Clark, Andrew Adonis, Andrew Cowan, Andrew Kidd, Brett Wigdortz, Chris Patten, Derek Johns, Jamie Byng, Jonathan Dimbleby, Julia Cleverdon, Julian Barnes, Kevin Prunty, Mark Haddon, Rona Kiley, Simon Jenkins, William Waldegrave, Zadie Smith.

Thanks to:
Arts Council England, Alice Jolly & Stephen Kinsella, Andrea Minton Beddoes & Simon Gray, The Anson Charitable Trust, The

Arvon Foundation, BBC Children in Need, BBC Radio 4 Appeal & Listeners, Beth & Michele Colocci, Big Lottery Fund, Blackwells, Boots Charitable Trust, Brunswick, Charlotte Hogg, Cheltenham Festivals, Clifford Chance, Danego Charitable Trust, First Editions Club Members, First Story Events Committee, Frontier Economics, Give A Book, Hollick Charitable Trust, Ink@84, Ivana Catovic of Modern Logophilia, Jane & Peter Aitken, John Lyon's Charity, John R Murray Charitable Trust, John Thaw Foundation, Lake House Charitable Foundation, Letters Live, Liz and Terry Bramall Foundation, Old Possum's Practical Trust, Open Gate Trust, Oxford University Press, Psycle Interactive, Robert Webb, Royal Society of Literature, Sigrid Rausing Trust, Sir Halley Stewart Trust, The Stonegarth Fund, Teach First, Tim Bevan & Amy Gadney, The Thomas Farr Charity, Walcot Foundation, Whitaker Charitable Trust, XL Catlin, our group of regular donors, and all those donors who have chosen to remain anonymous.

Most importantly we would like to thank the students, teachers and writers who have worked so hard to make First Story a success this year, as well as the many individuals and organisations (including those who we may have omitted to name) who have given their generous time, support and advice.

Contents

Introduction

Paula Rawsthorne

WRITER-IN-RESIDENCE

I was delighted to be invited to spend a second year as the First Story Writer-in-Residence for The Farnborough Academy. I was also delighted that many of last year's students wished to be involved again, as well as new recruits from different year groups. It's a testament to the students' commitment to and enjoyment of creative writing that we had Year Elevens (Dionne and Matthew) attending so many of the after-school sessions, despite all the pressure of their exam work. Dionne and Matthew have been part of the First Story group since it started at the school three years ago, and each year their writing gets stronger and stronger.

The weekly First Story workshops enable students to enjoy exploring their imaginations and developing their creative writing skills without any pressure. There's no homework, no grading and no assessments involved. The focus is on a relaxed and supportive environment where stories and poems can be conjured up and developed.

As was the case last year, the participating students have formed into a lovely, welcoming and inspiring group where everyone is listened to and encouraged. It's always fantastic to see the confidence of students growing throughout the weeks and months; this confidence doesn't just apply to the quality of their writing, but also to their ability to share their work and read out to the group. The students have also learnt the essential skill of a writer to review and edit their stories and poems until they are satisfied with what they have created.

One of a number of great opportunities offered to the First Story group is the chance to attend a week-long residential creative writing course. This takes place in an idyllic countryside retreat and offers the chance to meet other students from around the country and to work with professional writers and poets. I was so pleased when, last year, Dionne and Phoebe took up this opportunity and had an unforgettable time. They would encourage anyone to do the same, and I hope that The Farnborough Academy's students attending the residential this July will also find it a life-changing experience.

Once again, I would like to say a huge 'thank you' to Ms Slee, the school's dynamic librarian. She's the linchpin of the whole First Story operation at Farnborough and works tirelessly to ensure that the students get the most out of the programme. She does this role on top of all her other duties, including being such a champion of books and her mission to get the school reading.

I'd also like to thank Holly Hunkin from the University of Nottingham. Holly is a student who has been my 'shadow writer' during this First Story year. It has been great to have her on board, and I know that she's enjoyed working with the group.

All the students' creativity, talent and hard work can be found in their anthology *The Multiverses*. The title of the anthology was inspired by the fact that Stephen Hawking had recently died when we were debating a name for the book. We think Professor Hawking would have approved of the title – it's a good play on words, and we liked the image of sending our stories and poems out into the multiverse. We hope that you enjoy it!

Dear Your Majesty

Trinity Cooper

Dear Your Majesty,

Full disclosure, I want this job so badly I've learned *everything* about you, so I've got rid of every spider from your building and I've even posted guards to protect you from those creepy arachnids (should they return).

I'm hiring out Broadway for a year so that you can watch every musical whilst sitting in front-row seats.

I'm on my way to Dan and Phil's flat to bribe them to meet you *every* Saturday.

I plan to bring C. S. Lewis back from the dead and make him write more Narnia books *just for you!*

The top songs on your Spotify will be from *Wicked* and *Mamma Mia!* and you'll have your very own music channel exclusively for them.

Every Wednesday you'll have a dinner party with J. K. Rowling and Alan Turing. For the starter you'll have pizza with your favourite toppings, and for the main course you'll be served toad in the hole, which will be followed by a dessert of Turkish delight.

One day a week a silent orphan will watch *Peppa Pig* with you, and I promise that I'll always record your favourite films and TV shows, because you should be able to watch them whenever you wish.

You will never find another personal assistant like myself so *don't* make a mistake!

Yours truly,
Trinity Cooper

The Months

Trinity Cooper

December's party face was on, her little sister constantly pestering her, wondering whether it was her turn in the spotlight. It wasn't, of course, because everyone loved December. January was only loved by her one friend, February.

February was a strange girl with bubblegum-pink hair that always seemed to be messy and smelly. She only ever wore a pink pinafore with hundreds of pins scattered around it. She handed out chocolate and massive teddy bears everywhere she went. On the other hand, January had jet-black hair that she always wore in a tight bun. Wearing large black jumpers with grey jogging bottoms, and with her nails painted black, she gave off an aura of being cold-hearted, but everybody was wrong.

Anyway, it was the eve of December's big day. Her brunette hair was tied up in a plait. Her snowy-white skin was lost in a green flowing dress paired with maroon tights and a fluffy beige cardigan. There was a knock at the door. Her dark green jealous eyes widened. She ran downstairs, opening the oak doors to her mansion. Outside stood October and November, her two 'best friends'.

October had red hair that she always tied in pigtails, and wore a short orange dress that she paired with a cold frown. She had dark brown eyes that seemed soulless.

November was American. She had bright blue hair that she allowed to touch the floor. The colour of her hoodie matched her soft brown eyes, and she paired it with galaxy leggings. Even though she was the most optimistic of the group, she was still horrid.

But, despite their difference, all the girls had to get on, otherwise there would be no seasonal arrangement of time.

Family's Love

Trinity Cooper

The constant taunts and comic remarks
show that we love each other.
The tasty meal that's laid upon our plates
shows that we love each other.
The laughter that bellows out as we talk and joke
shows that we love each other.
The sarcastic way we reply
shows that we love each other.
We show our love in a different way to you.
It may be weird, but to us, it's ordinary.
I own my family's love and they own mine.
Our connection will never be severed.

I Own...

After Simon Armitage

Trinity Cooper

I do not own extroversion, which would allow me to talk to someone new without pausing and looking like an absolute idiot and to actually make a good joke, *jeez*!

But I do own a scar, proving I'm a lot braver than I think I am. This is my own unique way of showing that I'm different; and I don't just have one scar, but seven, because I'm a warrior.

I don't possess Dumbledore's wit, which would allow me to own his greatest quotes and deal with tense situations instead of crumbling under the weight.

But I do possess my own knowledge, which helps me get through a lot and, to me, that's all I need.

Idioms

Trinity Cooper

Cat got your tongue
When you forgot the lyrics you sung.

You blew my mind
With that joke that's one of a kind.

I threw in the towel
When I saw the dead body so foul.

I'm talking to a brick wall
When I give you a call.

I wore my heart on my sleeve
When *The Flash* had to leave.

I sent him away with a flea in his ear
But I was in fear because he was near.

J. K. Rowling drove me up the wall
When Sirius had to take that fall.

Darkness

Trinity Cooper

Dear Darkness,

Why do you engulf me in your sadness, tear me away from those
I love?

First my brother, now my wife.

You're the embodiment of beauty and jealousy

Contradicting each other every second.

You draw me in, but I push away, knowing it's wrong.

I feel like you're singling me out.

Tears don't stop when you leave your mark.

You act like you're an ally, but you're an enemy feeding others
my information,

Gaining joy out of my sadness.

I hope you like the cold iron bars that keep you away from me.

You will not break them.

Yours truly,

Charles

Love You with All My Heart

Kelsey Douglas-Walster

Love is everywhere, in the air and on the ground
Other people hate you, but I don't
Violins play gently as we eat
Everyone turns as you pass by
Your heart does so too
Others are not safe but
Under you I am
Who wouldn't love today?
I know I would
Today is the day
Hatred is gone
Always I am yours
Love is yours
Love is mine
My heart is with you
You and I are a good match
Hear those guitars playing our tune
Every day by the time of noon
Always near me holding me tight
Ready to hug me with all your might
Today, like every other day, you are mine.

My Bedroom

Kelsey Douglas-Walster

I see a broken bed in the middle of the room
Where I lay my head every day
And smell candy that tastes like bubblegum.
It never ends.
I hear cars outside my window
And touch cracks all over the walls and the roof.

La Vie en Paris

Dionne Goodman

'Bonjour,' I blurt out nervously to the garçon.

'Bonjour, mademoiselle, ça va?' he chirps back.

I gleam with pure ecstatic energy, baring my white canines at the man. I can smell the fresh bread baking. He hasn't looked up yet; he doesn't know me. I can't hold in my smile.

'Très bien, merci,' I say as he hands me the pain au chocolat and I hold out the money. He looks up, finally, to reach for the money, but jolts back with blunt force at the sight of my thin, pale fingers clutching the coins. He's noticed; my structure falls. I no longer stand tall with a smile, but now I feel small and weak and frail.

I raise my veil and his face stretches in complete terror, his eyes widen to bright torch lights and his mouth falls to form a gaping hole of questions and a forgotten scream.

I lift my arms to my mouth and bite the pain au chocolat and taste nothing. I've missed it – my taste – more than a person may miss a lover, in a sad, lonely sort of way. The bread drops through me and hits the ground. I watch the remains of it fall to my feet and pocket the rest for later. I drop my veil and shrink from the man's milk-pale face, bleached by fear.

I walk alone, alongside the Seine, followed by a trail of chocolate-covered breadcrumbs and an abundance of fearful cries and silent, peering eyes. I lower my face to the cracked stone trail, watching the crumbs fall from my pockets to the ground. I hear their gasps still, but focus my sight on the falling crumbs. Tears would form if they could, but my sadness still stabs like a stubborn child into my ribcage... hitting where my heart might once have been.

I turn my face towards the gaping crowd, teeth bared, eyes tired from the loneliness, features hollowed from the years. My bones shine in the light reflected from La Seine and La tour Eiffel. On the bridge there is only one way to go, so I raise my skeletal arms and fall softly to the water, wind coursing through my ribs and skull like I am part of it. Like a songbird in flight, I close my eyes and, for once, my bones feel human... for once, I feel alive, though I'm sure that I am not.

Selfish

Dionne Goodman

I do this odd thing, where I care and it makes me.
This warm butterfly in my chest that feels like a child's hope
in my lungs,
filling every breath with wonder and love.
And this feeling makes me complete.
It etches into me messages of selflessness, as if I am a leather-
bound book of scriptures, full with selfless words.
And when I am less than that, it rips the wings from the
butterfly and wears them in full, flamboyant outfits, blading its
name in my spine, screeching words of hatred into my skin.
I do this odd thing, where I care too much...
and it breaks me.

My Cinnamon Bronchioles

Dionne Goodman

I can feel it now, the deep warm burning on my tongue
That pulses like a beating heart in love with my stomach
And infatuates my senses, making me blind with heat.
The red seductress that fills the cold season with a light hiss,
Hot enough to melt snow, chilly enough to frost over the
    ground beneath.
The rising tangles of charred bark, iced on winter snow.
The cinnamon branches of my lungs burnt and old.
I hear it crackle in my chest, can smell its heat, feel its love.
In my lungs, in my cinnamon bronchioles,
There's a slight kiss of everything I love.

PA for the Day

Dionne Goodman

Dear Chloe,

After going through your important schedule, I have managed to input your meeting with Rihanna and Mia. I will arrange a coach, led by twelve pink horses, to take you to the Cullens' house by nine o'clock. The journey will take approximately five hours. I know that this is a long time, but I have provided a supply of sweets (excluding pineapple and those sickly-sweet mango ones that you detest so much).

Whilst screening *Frozen* and *Trolls* on your extremely high, magically comfortable coach, you will dine sophisticatedly, eating the most delectable chicken, sweetcorn and BBQ pizza and an unlimited supply of ice-cold Tizer.

On arrival at His Majesty's, Edward Cullen will escort you up the mountains of Oregon and, once downstream, you will run alongside the wolves to the cinema where an exclusive anime has been prepared for you. While you watch you'll consume sweet – *not* spicy – korma.

After that you'll be sent to the forest to play baseball with all the Cullen family. Mia and Rihanna against the X-Men and Justin Bieber. However, undefeated after three long games, a brawl will start between Rihanna and Justin. He'll be unconscious on the floor after one vital blow from Rihanna's ladylike fists. The X-Men, cheering the defeat, will invite you into their clan as the next Storm. You'll dance with glee like you're on *The Next Step*… anything is possible with me in your world.

Dionne

Jack O'Boy

Dionne Goodman

'A mind does wonders in a rough, hard shell,' you said, with a
    well-equipped head and a wit like a whip.
You remember years and dates like no other,
Like the birthdate of your sister's, husband's, father's brother.
You're the only one who can remember the name of the
    old-fashioned TV set you've had since you were twenty-six.
For years your heart is paced and brain is ready, then and now.
You're still going strong, a family man with a kind, sweet heart.
With buckets and buckets of photos,
Memories from the start of your history lay inside of your head,
Of the lost and found, history for you is not dead.
So remember your story, remember it all.
Remember the days we spent staring at the photographs
And conversing in beautiful tales of the young and old.
But, for our family, the apple did fall far from the tree, far from
    that space.
Jack O'Boy, Jack Rabbit, a Jack of all trades,
I will never forget those days.

The Foreigner

Dionne Goodman

Her mouth twisted foreign words into eloquent speeches,
Her tongue formed perfect dictations of new and ancient sounds
That gambolled through her mind into mine and straight back
out again.
The sentences lilted, coating my thoughts with thoughts of her
dulcet words
Encased in fleeting wonder.
It was if she had been a harbinger, and that I was to listen to
these words
Announced with a traveller's tongue
And take something from it.
A prophet in a way.
But her speech formed a gentle foreign breeze,
That I did not understand,
That I wish I had.

I Am What I Am

Avin Green

I am a potato, but not an ordinary potato
I mean a couch potato
Trying not to be a zombie blasted in a game
I'm a torch playing with flames
A tornado flying through the air
I am flowing water cos I never stop
I am the Leaning Tower of Pisa (not Pizza)
Cos I'm leaning for the top
Of the mountain that never stops
I am a gun ready to be cocked
Cos my trigger-fire is an explosive shock
I am what I am and it's fun to be me.

I Do Not Own…

After Simon Armitage

Avin Green

I do not own a gaming PC
But I do own a laptop where I can browse the internet and see
them get built on YouTube.
I do not own a dog
But I do have a kitten which is cute and doesn't need to go
for walks.
I do not own an Xbox One
But I do own an Xbox 360 which has ten times the amount
of games.
I do not own a car
But I do have legs which I can walk with.
I do not own a mansion
But I do have a flat that is cosy and a family that is close.

The Day I Wanted Everything to Go My Way

Avin Green

I knew I couldn't lie
When I nearly died
Cos of the smells that I cannot describe.
One of them a dinner on a plate
One of them was the smell of clickbait
One was the smell of things that didn't really go well
Cos my computer went into meltdown when it was left out in
the sun.
And for a year that stench didn't go away.
It left a corpse of a game named *State of Decay*
When on that same day
I wanted everything to go my way
Until my Xbox blew up
And I knew it wasn't going to be okay.

My Bedroom

Lyosha Hopkinson

My bedroom is a sweet-smelling heaven.
The air tastes of cookies when my wax burner is on.
It feels like I'm eating cotton candy every time I walk into
the room.
I am a laminate-lover with a rug on the floor as soft as a sheep,
I have a wild wolf on my wall who watches over me when
I sleep.
Come in and you shall see me in my castle.

Big Bad Wolf

Holly Hunkin

I feared a wolf had skinned you, torn out your insides, worn
    your face as a mask,
Until I stumbled out of that house of horrors and saw you'd
    been the wolf all along.
Your eyes were always wide, wild, ravenous;
Your fangs always aching to tear at my flesh, and I was blind
    to it.
Playing the part of harmlessness, you ate away at me,
Teeth sinking deeper with each bite.
And still I waited, forgiving, hoping the real you might resurface,
Worrying you never would.
I was afraid of the wrong thing.
I should have feared you sooner.

False Alarm

Holly Hunkin

Nothing's burning.
I promise nothing's burning.
There's no fire; I'm no arsonist.
So why are you screaming?

The tiniest wisp of steam and the fire alarm goes off.
Without warning, the piercing siren shrieks through the house.
All I can do is cower at the sound,
Cover my ears and pray for the clamour to end;
I can't get close enough to the alarm to turn it off without it
    deafening me.
So, I wait it out, my face wrapped in a pillow to smother
    the sound.
Eventually the siren stops and the silence is blissful,
But the echo still reverberates in my ears, unshakable for days.

Just when I start to wonder if maybe I'm safe, the screaming
    starts again.
The fire alarm keeps wailing out of the blue,
Until I'm afraid to put the kettle on, blow out birthday candles,
Or open the bathroom door after a hot shower,
Lest the rush of steam set it off again.

I've started to be braced for it whenever I'm in the house,
Just in case I do some little thing wrong and trigger the alarm.
But no amount of being ready for it stops me jumping.
I didn't want to take the batteries out,

But at this point, smoke inhalation is more appealing than being
    roused in the middle of the night by another screaming fit.

Sometimes I wonder if I should just douse the curtains in
    lighter fluid
And turn the house to ash,
Because the siren will sound no matter what I do,
And I'm so tired...

I've moved house since then
And the fire alarm here doesn't go off for no reason.
I'm still waiting for it, though.

Love of My Life

After John Cooper Clarke

Holly Hunkin

I'll be the crumpled tenner in your pocket
you didn't know you had.
I'll be the fuel to your space rocket,
lift you up off your launchpad.
I'll be the Cillit Bang to clean your mould,
your Kleenex when you have a cold.
With you, my darling, I'm gonna grow old.

I'll be your black-out blinds,
so you can sleep a little later.
You and me, we're intertwined;
you're the top to my denominator.
When you crash, I'll be your back-up drive.
Your defibrillator, darling I'll revive you.
I'll love you as long as I'm alive.

I'll be your fancy moisturiser,
seal up all your cracks.
On a sunny day, I'll be your visor.
You're the cheese to my mac.
When you come in to land, I'll be your runway.
At the end of the week, I'll be your Sunday.
I'll love you, darling, till we're old and grey.

A Single Heartbeat for You

Matthew Isaac

Following the blood and decay in the air,
A combined taste of bad luck and evil,
A quiet silence, slowly approaching,
Every drop of sweat a seed of fear.
Like a fish to a lure,
My curiosity leading the sanity of my soul
To the misery of its destruction.
Twigs snapping like bones
As I get closer and closer.
But the answers emanate from within.
A body engulfed in flies
Only inspires my traumatised mind.
A figure emerges,
My adrenaline hard at work
And my heart causing earthquakes at each beat –
Blink!

Crab Sticks

Matthew Isaac

A stripy stall ahead of us,
Somehow shining out from the rest.
I walk towards it, hypnotised,
And from it I'm handed a peculiar food.
I handle it like a gem.
Without hesitation I devour it instantly
But then,
Every cell screaming,
Hard at work,
My stomach has a revolution against it.
Its taste is a revolting, bitter, salty poison.
I try to keep it down
But everything screams, 'NO!'
Like a bullet from a gun
It shoots out uncontrollably.
My sister is not impressed,
Dripping in vomit.

The Unexpected

Matthew Isaac

I board the train with a blissful feeling.
The clouds are shifting,
The train is departing.
Its steam cheers, coughing, sneezing, talking.
The ticket inspector approaches
But is never there.
The lights flicker in a never-ending pattern
But darkness falls when we enter the tunnel.
A cold figment passes by.
The burning in Hell can be heard,
A freezing burning Hades is running through the carriages,
Children's laughter transformed into tears.
The cold chill whispers away.
The train exits the tunnel, only to reveal...

Creepy Santa

Matthew Isaac

It was all such a wonderful time. Everyone would laugh and play.
Presents would be exchanged in front of me throughout the day,
But little did I know the years have been filled with lies,
As their innocence dies.
However, on one snowy night, such deception I heard,
Hate towards me which was thicker than my beard.
Please remember the last decade we had together –
I may be smashed and have a broken back,
But I carry lots of memories in my missing sack.

I Am Who I Am Because...

Matthew Isaac

Who? No...
What would I be without *The Eleventh Hour*
The games I enjoy playing
The genes that contain me
The heart that sustains me
The wonderful, sometimes creepy, friends I know
The dreams of being the last one standing in the catacombs
The buses I have been under
The exaggerations and lies (I'm full of)
And, of course, the fish fingers and custard that tempt my
    stomach to turn
And turn dreams to nightmares?

PA for the Day

Phoebe Lees

Dear Boi 100,

After recently discovering your advertisement requesting applications for a PA, I've decided to write to you because I believe that I would be perfect for the job. Why? Well, if you read on, I shall tell you.

First of all, I'd hire the best-trained janitor ever, to make sure that there would never, ever be a hair on your toilet for as long as you live.

I'd also secretly arrange with NASA to banish Team 10 to Pluto ASAP; trust me when I say I find them incredibly annoying and undeserving of the attention they get.

I'd guarantee that on every single birthday you have, I'd recreate the time that you were at Flaming Dragon on your tenth birthday when your friend, Dylan, failed at eating chips with chopsticks.

As I know how much you despise anime, I'd make sure to burn every single copy of every anime ever created (and probably enjoy it). Furthermore, I know you're a big fan of Neil Patrick Harris, so I'd arrange for you both to meet and to high-five each other.

I happen to have heard how much you like Shaq and, if you hired me, I'd get in touch with him so you two can have a photoshoot to appear together on a poster.

You would no longer have to hear, or see, any *Real Housewives* series ever again, because I'd personally get a law passed forbidding them from being televised, and I wouldn't forget about giving you the powers of Shazam!

Now, on to the way to your heart – FOOD! I'd make sure you can get a bucketful (though not provided in an actual bucket) of breaded chicken fillets whenever you desire.

I hope that this unique, totally amazing, one-of-a-kind, brilliant and incredible application convinces you to hire me.

Yours sincerely,

Phoebe

The God of Spreads

Phoebe Lees

I sit here, as I write about you, in the presence of your holy spirit sent from above. I admit, when I first tried your amazing chocolatey grace on a slice of slightly crispy toast… I thought of you as an enemy. I did not appreciate you as I do now. In fact, it was a few years before I was in your presence again. You were spread across the small, smooth pancakes that I decided I absolutely needed to snack upon. Your neighbouring pancake was smothered in jam. A slightly strange combination, but it no longer matters, as you are now the only spread that I allow to go near my pancakes.

When I took the first bite, it was a blessing to my tastebuds. An explosion of chocolate better than any other spread. Never had I tasted anything so extraordinary. I began worshipping you from that day onwards.

Whenever I see you sitting upon the shelves of a shop, I immediately grab and embrace you, setting you down on a pillow of crisps in the safety of the trolley. Once home, you take your extremely well-earned place on your throne. Your royal minions of various canned and bottled food surrounding you, practically kissing your feet.

You are a god. The God of Spreads.

Nutella, I shall forever worship you.

Explosive

Phoebe Lees

I am November. I am not happy. I am never happy.

Everyone's so ridiculously loud and I hate it with a capital 'H'!

Everyone wants me to celebrate but NO!

They all call me cold-hearted for brushing them all off, but can you blame me?

They only associate me with fire and rebellion.

It's not my fault Parliament was almost blown to smithereens. It was my brother!

It was Guy's fault!

But they blame me, saying, 'Oh November, your personality is so explosive, it must've been you.'

It was not me, but my image probably doesn't help.

I tend to slip into the shadows to hide how I truly feel.

I'm dark. I'm cold. I'm bitter.

So what?

It's not like January is much different!

Why don't they all talk about him?

Why's it always November this, November that. 'November's evil!'

'I'm not!' I scream, but they still don't stop.

I snap at them. They go quiet for a few hours. Then they insult my anger.

I can never win.

Why can't I be like October – ignored?

No. November with the explosive personality.

Always tease her until she snaps.

They always remember, remember to tease November.

I Own Netflix (Not Literally)

Phoebe Lees

I own Netflix. Well, not literally, but I have a subscription.

Well, technically it's my mum's subscription, but my name is on one of the profiles!

It's obviously the best one out of my sister's, my mum's, and the oldies'.

I have the best watch history, honestly.

Shows like *Shadowhunters*, *Teen Wolf*, *Godless* and *RuPaul's Drag Race* are all on there.

Everyone else's history is a total bore! *Once Upon a Time*, *Only Fools and Horses*, *Prison Break*. Who needs them?

But I guess, I have to admit, the choice is broad.

So, Netflix is pretty good (totally not an understatement to hide my not-so-secret obsession).

However, it's a huge disappointment when there are too many people watching.

Oh, and I *do not* appreciate Netflix judging me for binge-watching show for hours –

'Are you still watching?'

Of course I am! I would've turned it off if I wasn't.

Utterly ridiculous!

Blind Spot

Phoebe Lees

Discarded. Ignored. Alone.

He sits next to the busiest restaurant in town, yet everyone passes him, attracted to the sweet, perfected tunes of the accordion across from him. He's forced into a corner, a corner of society's outcasts. He gets no pity, he gets no sympathy. All he receives from his lifestyle is the feeling of invisibility.

Some children dream of having the superpower to become invisible but, if they knew the reality, their dreams would become nightmares. The musician that plays across the street blinds the customers heading to the restaurant; they all stand and watch as he suffers. He even welcomes them, encouraging them to enter the restaurant, but to them, he may as well be a mouse.

A word, or even a smile, could make his life the tiniest bit brighter, but no, he's left to sit there like a forgotten coffee cup. He no longer feels the love he once had for life, or the hope to get through it. He just sits there.

Discarded. Ignored. Alone.

A Day You'll Love or Hate

Phoebe Lees

Vermin crawling over each other.
Atrocious displays of poxy love.
Lonely suckers left to hate.
Every card shop is basking in gullible lovers.
Never a minute without the dreaded, 'Who's your valentine?'
Together forever, all the cards claim. Just wait till next
  Valentine's to rid your delusions.
Intrusions from weak old couples acting in love.
No spaces left in any restaurant; all are reserved for doomed
  dates.
Energy is wasted on pathetic poems written in a minute.
Spoken love confessions that reek of future rejection.
Destined-to-fail relationships go strong for one day only.
Another excuse to beg for presents.
You can never manage to get away from the apparent *celebration*,
  as ridiculous as it is.

May

Crystal Mann-Bolam

I am May and I pretend to be so happy.
With my golden hair, blonde eyebrows and hazel eyes.
Sometimes I feel left out because all the other months are better
than me.
They all have better holidays than mine.

May Day isn't so great.
November has Bonfire Night and December has Christmas.
Why can't I have a fun holiday? Why?
I spend all my time making sure that it's perfect, but no one
appreciates it.
I try my best to brighten things up, but all my sorrow becomes
rain.
Yes, there are birthdays to look forward to, but they turn my
happiness to sadness, knowing that everything will fade away,
Leaving me alone again, as dreams are fading.
I have no friends to talk to about anything.
I once thought that July liked me,
But when I spoke to her she just ignored me.
Once I heard and felt the warmth of July singing all day.
So, I called out to her, 'What are you doing here?'
She turned her back on me, shouting, 'I am better than you!'
Then it started to rain with all my sorrow coming upon me.
It's not my fault that I only have one holiday, which no one is
bothered about.
I wish I could be popular, but that would take a miracle.

I try my best; wear a bright daisy dress and a soft blue cardigan,
Trying to look like spring and hope.
But I'm just a loner.
A month with one stupid holiday.

I May Not Own...

After Simon Armitage

Crystal Mann-Bolam

I may not own a unicorn teddy, because it's too expensive,
But I do own my life, so I can break free whenever I want.
I'm not able to own a sheep, because they're hard to keep,
But I do own my ex's phone number.
I may not own a bed in school, so I can sleep instead of work,
But I do own my personality.
I'm not able to own a whiteboard, like the one at school,
    because I can't afford it,
But I do have all of my glitter pens at home.
I'm not able to own high heels, because I'm too young,
But I do have better shoes to wear (that I can actually walk in).
I may not have a cat, but I do have a dog
And at least the dog lets me take him for walks.
I may not own crystals, because they're expensive,
But I do have my name, which is priceless.

I Love You

Crystal Mann-Bolam

I'm seriously in love with you, but I might be too stupid for you.
Love is pretend anyway.
Once upon a time I was lovesick, but now I'm over the
Virus that flows through my heart and the
Enemies that destroy out of jealousy.
You're powerless to do anything
Other than die of sorrow.
Using people is sad, especially if you think about them all
the time.

My Bedroom

Crystal Mann-Bolam

It's strange that I see cleanliness even though my grandma
    doesn't.
I feel the thick, silky softness of my quilt, as soft as fluff,
And taste the candy handles of my wardrobe.
I hear the *Harry Potter* theme tune welcoming me when I walk
    through the door.
I see *Harry Potter* posters everywhere, filling my bedroom,
And smell the sweetness of happy times behind and ahead of me.

I Am What I Am Because...

Syntych Mayala

My mum loves me
I love travelling around the world
I am never stable
I am loving and caring deep inside
I am '*that*' girl
I am the annoying sister who has the most chores
I am a lucky girl to have a best friend like no other
I am grateful to have the family I have
I am the Eiffel Tower, forever looking over Paris
And the girl screaming on Space Mountain
I am the glue of the family, never letting us break
I am who I am and I love what I am!

Chips and Chicken

Bella Nwaneto

Chips and Chicken, great mates.
Burger and Chicken, great rivals.
Fought for the hand of Chips.
Chicken seasoned himself every day
And Burger changed his sauce.
But one fine McDonald's day, Chips declared that neither of
them reached her expectations.
Burger's seeds fell off
And Chicken's crispy parts crumbled.
They were heartbroken.
But they were bound to spice their way through everything.
Two years later, Chicken was in a terrible way, going to
commit a burning mistake,
About to be eaten in KFC.
Burger ran in, all his toppings falling off, and rescued him.
Luckily their mutual, undying love for Chips saved the day.
Hooray for fries!

My Bedroom

Bella Nwaneto

My room is noisy, like cars beeping in traffic but
Run your hands through the carpet and you'll feel it's the jungle
Where we're always jumping on the beds like monkeys.
Because of this you'll smell new furniture that's replaced what
    we've damaged.
You'll smell burgers and chips lingering uncontrollably in the
    air, because we're always sneaking them upstairs.
And the first thing you'll see when you walk in is a television,
    facing the bed, showing *Dancing with the Stars*, waiting for
    them to fall over, so I can end my day with a laugh.

The Yet-to-Be-Tasted Pizza

Bella Nwaneto

Juicy, mouth-watering, thin crust pepperoni pizza!
Eavesdropping on my mum while she was ordering
And interrupting her phone call to add more and more layers of
toppings.
My mouth pouring like a river because I couldn't control my
thirst for pizza.
Mum told me to calm down,
But when it arrived, the smell of it wouldn't stop bugging me
till I finally gave in
And I chucked every last piece of it in my mouth
But with a side dip of guilt,
Because I knew what kind of trouble I'd be in when I was done.

Without the Star

Bella Nwaneto

If you throw me away I won't complain.
Just note to self, life without me won't be the same.
Think of all those shared memories we have.
I'm practically your whole Christmas.
Without me, you're like a horse without a saddle,
A hand without a glove,
Santa without a beard,
Rudolph without his red nose.
So, think twice before you throw *this* star away.
Without me you'll fall apart.
It will be like you, without your heart.

Scared Straight

Jane Nwaneto

Coming into a new school was such a fright.
I tried to make things right.
But no matter how hard I tried, nothing good was in sight.
Some people used to fight
But I knew that wasn't right.
I miss my bestie.
She was so messy
But she always had my back,
Even though she done bad,
Which made me really sad,
But oh, that was in the past.
She's my number one,
She's my ride or die
And she was always real.
Then I moved away and nothing was the same
And I just wanted to cry
Baby girl,
You're the only one!

These Tings

Jane Nwaneto

You make me laugh,
You make me sad,
Even though I feel like trash.
You got all your main tings.
You got all your fake tings.
Even though you fully brag.
You like to cause drama.
You like to cause stress.
You're like all the rest.
You're like unsalted bacon
With all its plain flavours.
Even though you're second best.
Your friends are so funny
Even though they're all like honey.

I Am What I Am

Jane Nwaneto

I am what I am because I'm strong, independent and hopeful about what will happen in the future.

When I was younger I used to move around a lot, and it was hard for me to make new friends as I wouldn't be able to keep them for long.

When I was younger, I used to be very shy and didn't speak much, but now I've been influenced by people who have had to overcome their fears and I have built up my confidence by seeing their courage.

When once I went on a five-day trip, I wasn't keen on participating in the activities, but I became more confident and was able to join in with everything and stay positive through the rest of the days.

The last thing I'd like to say is that I love chicken!

Dear Millie

Ella Richardson

Dear Millie,

I would be delighted to be your personal assistant, and I guarantee that you would never ever, *ever* find another personal assistant like me in the whole galaxy.

During my research I found that you were petrified of spiders and zombies. Well, lucky for you, *I'm* absolutely fine with everything. So, I will capture every single spider and slay all the zombies for you.

I'll also get all the Frankie & Benny's in the world just for you to try, and then banish the foods you hate; especially those vile vegetables, broccoli and Brussels sprouts. And, don't worry, I'll make sure that you'll always have your two favourite things with you – unicorns and Cadbury chocolate. The most beautiful unicorn will sleep at the end of your bed at night, and together you can chomp on your lifetime supply of Cadbury Caramel.

Of course, as your personal assistant, I'll be able to make your dreams come true. In fact, Emma Watson and Luke Evans are on their way to have the most exquisite dinner with you. In the spare room I've already set up the karaoke machine for you all to sing your favourite song together, 'Fine Line', and, I just have to say, I think you sing it way better.

So that's why I think I would be best for the job; I'm not scared of anything and I already know so many things about you, and if you hire me I will get straight on with the work you give me.

Yours hopefully,
Ella Richardson

July, June's Big Sister

Ella Richardson

July walks through the meadow with her arms outstretched.
Her soft pink dress trails over the flowers
Whilst the summer breeze sweeps through her hair;
Long and fine, light blue fading into aqua green.
The sun shines three times brighter every time July looks upon it
With her golden eyes,
Making everyone joyful, including the forest animals.
The birds and squirrels climb all over her arms,
But there's one person who July can never make happy
And that's her younger sister, June.
June is not who you think.
She might be considered the first month of summer
But she's not jolly or sunny.
She's a goth who only leaves her bedroom to eat and go to
    the bathroom.
Her room is all black except one white pillow.
No one knows the real June, deep down, except June herself.
She's never told anyone that she's actually a study nerd.
She loves to study, but she's worried the truth will make her
    less popular.

Angel

Ella Richardson

Angel, my angelic Staffy.
Eyes like hazelnuts.
White chest, surrounded by prickly dark brown fur,
So tough it's like stroking sandpaper,
Like pricking your finger on a cactus.
And don't get me started on how hyper she is.
Since Angel was a pup, she's been
Biting the noses off teddies,
Jumping up at us every morning,
Pushing the settee as far back as it will go.
I can't even get through *Hollyoaks*
Without Angel collapsing on me like a ton of bricks.
But I wouldn't be complete without her,
Because I love her,
And I can tell she loves me.

Valentine's Day

Ella Richardson

Violins swirling in the air.
A waterfall of memories falling on us.
Love is in our heart.
Eyes widened from love at first sight.
Nothing is better than you in my life.
Teddies from you are like sunshine for the first time.
I can't stop the butterflies when you walk by.
Now I proclaim my endless love.
Ears long to hear the words 'I love you' from your mouth.
Sometimes we fight, but it won't impact on our love.
Don't let weird things about us split us apart.
Altogether, love will live forever.
You're the apple of my eye.

Librarian's Valentine

Ms Slee

I am checking you out

Library card in hand
Oh, how excited am I?
Various reviews hold promise
Every last one positive

Yearning for my bed
Ovaltine is made
Under my duvet, finally, with my book

PA for the Day

Millie White

Dear Ella,

My name is Millie and I'm delighted to inform you that I will be ecstatic to be your very own personal assistant for the whole day. I will be devastated if you don't choose me, because I can assure you that you will never find another assistant like me in the rest of the universe.

I know that you absolutely love Chinese bread so I will fly you, first class, all the way to Gran Canaria, just to get a lifetime supply of it, together with strawberries and raspberries, which I know you also love.

I also guarantee to provide Jacqueline Wilson and David Walliams books, which I believe you adore.

I will ban all the Brussels sprouts and bananas just for you, because you hate them ever so much.

I will personally cage all types of spiders as I realise you're petrified of them, thinking that they suck the blood of humans.

I will make sure that you will be the first person to time-travel, just so that you can see what you do in the future (i.e. pick me!).

I will imprison The Trip at school so he can learn his lesson, and I'll show him up by standing up to him in front of everyone.

Finally, I will make sure you break the world record for the largest teddy bear collection.

I look forward to hearing that I've got the job.

Yours sincerely,

Millie White

Fake Mistletoe

Millie White

How dare you!

Who do you think you are, thinking about getting rid of me?

Oh, if I told you all the secrets I know, you would definitely
keep me for generations to come.

That real mistletoe will die within weeks, and would poison
you with its berries given half a chance.

I have hung here Christmas after Christmas and I plan to stay
for many more.

I was above you for the *first kisses* of, not only you, but your
parents and grandparents too.

I can make love last FOREVER,

And I can last forever, my powers never fading.

So, keep me or you'll regret it.

Keep me or love will die. #Cruel.

I Do Not Own...

After Simon Armitage

Millie White

I do not own a dance studio

But I do own a place where I can dance to my heart's content, listening to my favourite songs.

I do not own a sheep

But I do own a woolly dog to keep me warm when she sits on my knees when it's cold outside.

I do not own a fluffy bunny

But I have two brothers who make me feel like the greatest person in the world when I feel like the worst.

I do not own a big mansion

But I'm proud to say that I have a small house that feels like the world's greatest home, because that's where my heart is!

Dear Sunshine

Eliza Widdowson

Dear Sunshine,

We've been way too out of touch. Things have been crazy and it sucks that we don't talk that much. But I should tell you that I'm the best choice for this job because, if I were your personal assistant, I would start your day by exterminating every spider within a five-mile radius.

I would then purchase a unicorn from Morrisons, personally searching the biscuit aisle for however long it takes. Then, I would use its unicorn powers to teleport you to the YouTube HQ to meet Alan Turing and J. K. Rowling before getting you a VIP pass to Comic-Con.

After that you'll meet Dan and Phil and Harry Hart, followed by a screening of *Grease* and *Dirty Dancing* where you'll be accompanied by Sirius and Regulus Black. Then you'll have an enchanting time with witches, eating pineapple and pizza.

On Fridays, Sky One will only show *Sherlock* and *The Flash*, back to back, while you eat all kinds of FREE chocolate.

I will book out *Planet Bounce* and *Laser Quest* just for you, so you can have a private day of bouncing and shooting. After this fun day you'll go to the theatre and watch *Dear Evan Hansen* while Justin Bieber is imprisoned. Taron Egerton will give you an acting workshop in *Star Lab* before you obtain the power of super-speed.

With this, you'll catch the Hogwarts Express and be able to read or listen to anything *except TWILIGHT*! Curry will be off the menu on the train and, while having your relaxing journey, Queen will play for you until you reach your destination.

After a personal tour of the school with Teddy Lupin, you'll go back on the Hogwarts Express whilst reading any JohnLock fanfiction you desire.

Sincerely,

Eliza

P.S. I guarantee that if you give me the job I will also never tell anyone your 'DEMON CHILD' secret.

Epoch Enclave

Eliza Widdowson

December was beautiful, seen as special, and everybody felt drawn to her. But, underneath her jolly exterior, she was cold and bitter. She seemed the life of every party. Her red hair swished and her make-up glittered. She outshone everyone, especially her sister, January.

Always in December's shadow, January had no problem hiding her cold heart. Bleached white hair and a (way too big) wooly jumper engulfed her entirely.

She always convinced people to do things that she knew they would never achieve; promoting the gym as much as she could, then laughing in their faces when they failed.

January's only friend, February, was a hopeless romantic. Handing out cookies and stuffed bears to everybody was basically a tradition.

She and her boyfriend, March, enjoyed coffees and snuggly sweaters. They loved to stay in, reading.

On the other hand, April would rain on everyone's parade. He wore his long hair in a blue bun, ruining plans and slouching in dark corners.

May was studious with messy hair (no time to brush it). And dark circles under her eyes (no time to sleep). Always taking and retaking tests, which was somewhat unnecessary due to her As (but she required A*s). Nobody ever caught her outside.

June and his boyfriend, July, were complete opposites. June was tall and lanky with a long fringe and plain Converse shoes. He was always worried, but July calmed him down.

July wore massive hoodies and obnoxious flashing-LED Heelys; he was a literal human furnace. June would lean on him as much as he could.

August was chill. He was smaller than everyone else, but sassier than them, if they tested him. He did nothing with any strong emotion, but his free nature attracted many friends.

Nobody was as confused as September. She tried to study hard, failing miserably, and getting lost on the way to classes, having to ask for help from October, who was always wandering around the corridors with his black coat over his blazer and his heavy eyeliner.

November was forgotten. She sat in the corner of the library, drowning her sorrow in true magic and worlds she wished she was part of.

Not-So-Fantastic Fidelity

Eliza Widdowson

Hands link,
Eyes meet.
Any hug of yours
Radiates heat –
This is a love no one can beat.

Violets to my door,
As if I hadn't told you before
Love is not what I feel for you,
Everything's not a game for two.
No feelings take over my heart.
Teddies don't fill up my shopping cart.
Is this too much to say?
No love I had for you anyway.
Every book could beat you any day.

Loving awkwardly
Over the mahogany table,
Very aware their parents have made them spend
Each and every day together, they'll never mend.

Six-Word Stories

Eliza Widdowson

Obsessed with him. Meet him. Meh.

Wish I could meet fictional characters.

You, me, wedding. You, me, lawyers.

Blanked by Prince. Cinderella home alone.

Watched musical. Now singing never-ending – sorry.

Books house more magic than wands.

Ann hid behind wall. Betrayed. Caught.

Orchestrina

Eliza Widdowson

They were roaming around the manor, letting their braces fall to their sides; there was no point in looking smart, and the trousers kept up anyway.

Peter and Noel took the lead as Anthony stayed behind. Every step he took was tentative, scared to get caught or break something. He looked around curiously at the pictures on the wall and stopped at a particularly strange one: a girl with pale skin and white hair doing a pirouette. Anthony peered over his shoulder to point out the painting to the others, but they were gone.

'Pete? Noel?' he called. No response. The boy sighed, rolling his eyes and wondering where they'd gone.

Behind Anthony was a large door with a lion head doorknob and flowery patterns spanning the walls. Too enchanted to walk away, Anthony reached for the doorknob and, turning, pushed it hard. As the door squealed open, he stepped inside and gasped at the sight. A colossal ballroom lay before him, windows spanning the two walls next to him and revealing a dark garden; all plants long dead and withered. The windows let in so much light, the sun reflected off the marble floor and Anthony felt heat burning in his hair.

Then he looked up. A large, open music box stood at the end of the hall. A life-sized ballerina spun slowly to hypnotic piano music.

Biographies

Trinity Cooper

Trinity, oh, where do we start with this one? This optimistic fool believes that love conquers hatred. Aside from that, she's become far too attached to fictional characters and is constantly attacked by her family's questions about why she's crying over people who don't exist – but they just don't understand.

Harry Potter may have his scar, but she has her ear dents. If this Hufflepuff could meet just one person it would probably be J. K. Rowling, even though she wouldn't know what to say to her.

Kelsey Douglas-Walster

Kelsey is an animal-loving Ravenclaw who's obsessed with *Harry Potter* just like her auntie and her best friend, even though her friend is a Hufflepuff. She has autism (though she doesn't know what it means). Kelsey's ambition is to be a maths teacher and she has a few secrets that will stay hers forever. Her favourite foods include spaghetti bolognese and pizza.

Dionne Goodman

Hi! My name's Dionne. I love reading and am obsessed with *Harry Potter*, EVERYTHING about *Harry Potter*… SLYTHERIN RULES! I play ukulele and write – mainly poems, but I do enjoy writing short stories sometimes. I wish to bestow upon you some words of wisdom – 'Don't be afraid to give up the good, to go for the great.'

Avin Green

Hello world, my name is Avin Green or, as people know me, 'The Gun Game Master' (that name comes from a very popular game called *Call of Duty*). I like to go to First Story to get away from real life and make my imagination go wild – I could be falling from a building, climbing a rock wall to the top of the biggest mountain in the world, or just playing a game that hasn't even come out yet – yes, I am hating on the game developers, but still, I can't make games as I am only fourteen, but I can write poems and stories, so that's a plus.

Lyosha Hopkinson

Lyosha is a quiet, yet loud, character. She's always on the go. If you try to catch her you won't succeed because, in the blink of an eye, she's off! At first you think she's quiet, but then you turn around and she's jumping about on the table like a monkey, like she hasn't been to the jungle gym. She has a tiger for a brother and a meerkat for a sister.

Holly Hunkin

Taker of naps and maker of terrible puns, Holly is a second-year student of English and Creative Writing at the University of Nottingham who is not short, but *fun size*, and dreams of one day becoming a publisher (or at least hopefully not working in retail). Her talents include baking, inhaling enough mac and cheese to feed a small family, and crying at videos of kittens on the internet because their little pink jelly bean toes are, *sniffle*, just so cute.

Matthew Isaac

Matthew Isaac is a weird and… well, he's just a weird person; he loves chocolate and chicken nuggets but not together; the genotype for his eye colour is homozygous. He hates physics and viral pathogens, but mainly physics. His knowledge of buses has no blockade, and, ladies and gentlemen and you, the reader, that is… that has been Matthew Isaac.

Phoebe Lees

Phoebe… yes, her AGAIN. The one who gets way too into TV shows and movies. She definitely didn't cry in the cinema whilst watching *The Death Cure*, no, not at all. She may, or may not, have two thousand photos in her gallery currently (probably more), which totally doesn't contradict her goal of not getting too attached to fictional characters.

Crystal Mann-Bolam

Crystal is an animal-loving Hufflepuff who adores *Harry Potter* and loves writing all the time. She's always scribbling while watching HP. She talks to her friends to get ideas, but sometimes she can be silly and kind. This Hufflepuff can be dangerous, so watch out!

Syntych Mayala

Syntych, how do I put this, well… she is the most annoying, bigmouthed girl you could ever meet, but she is also the most loyal, caring, worthy softy you could ever know. Be nice, because she will be curing you next; you don't know what she's capable of. If she had powers, she would have the cure for cancer. If she could go anywhere in the world, it would be Florida.

Bella Nwaneto

Bella is like a bell: you never know when she's going to ring. She's that one person who causes chaos in the deadest of silences. She is like a broken fire alarm because she never goes off. If you ever need a party planner, just call her, but be aware that she'll certainly turn the party on. Although she's not perfect, she's always planning big dreams that you'll least expect. Remember her name because this girl don't play the blame game, because everyone knows she can't be tamed.

Jane Nwaneto

Jane is great! She is strong and clever but fun too! If she was to change something, she would change the way people see things, like books for example. Jane would hope that everyone's imagination was as wild and daft as her own. She would also make sure that there is always something for everyone to do, so no one's ever bored or feeling down. Jane would make sure that everyone has the wildest dreams – dreams that are peaceful but magnificent.

Paula Rawsthorne

Paula Rawsthorne is extremely lucky to have her dream job of making up stories and teaching creative writing to wonderful students. Whilst watching *Escape to the Country* she becomes seduced by the idea of living in the countryside but, in reality, she knows that she'd be bored silly after two weeks and crave the hustle and bustle of the city.

Ella Richardson

Ella's dreams are to cook and write and she's going to be the best, as she's always serving up the best ideas. But, I'm warning you, don't wake her up early as she's a night owl who's in love with Ferrero Rocher. When you get to know her, you'll find that she's funny and kind and also won an award for being 'An Unsung Hero'.

Oh, and don't tell a joke around her because she'll laugh so hard that she'll turn red, because anything, I mean *anything*, will make her laugh. Don't sit on her throne in front of the TV, because it's the best seat to watch her favourite shows. However, as soon as the sports or horror come on, it's like she disappears.

Ms Slee

Ms Slee isn't 'just a librarian'; she's a kickass ninja warrior, thwarting the attempts of those teens that claim books are boring to mean it. Her expertise is matching books to people, sending them on the adventures of their lives and blowing their minds. When she's not combating literary apathy, she loves nothing more than a nice cup of tea and a sit down.

Millie White

Millie... she likes to think that she sings better than all the professionals, when really, she sings like a dying cat – MEOWCH! She also thinks she can write like J. K. Rowling, but her stories make no sense. Even J. K. Rowling wouldn't be able to rewrite Millie's work to make it into a story (don't say you heard this from me) ☺ Is she better than everyone else? Maybe, maybe not. But, in my honest opinion, she hangs around with a bunch of great people that she calls 'friends'. When she's at school all she does is stare into space; come on, I mean… WHO DOES THAT? Well, unless you are, of course, MILLIE WHITE.

Eliza Widdowson

Eliza, yes, the girl who was born purple and gets way too involved in fictional characters. She's obsessed with *Harry Potter* and just about any musical out there. This is why she wants to tread the boards when she's older, mostly wanting to play characters with ridiculous names like Penny Pingleton, Wednesday Addams, Racetrack Higgins and Elphaba Thropp. She won't shut up about *Harry Potter* and has a lot of Hufflepuff pride, but don't mention the *Newsies*, unless you want an hour-long speech on how much she loves it, but wishes that there weren't only three female characters. If you want to find her, just look for the girl blubbering in the corner of the school library due to the death of Riff and Bernardo… but not Tony!

The Gate Theat

CU00819366

The World Premiere of

UNBROKEN

By ALEXANDRA WOOD
Inspired by Arthur Schnitzler's LA RONDE

First performed at the Gate Theatre, London on 5 February 2009

The Gate Theatre is supported by

UNBROKEN
By ALEXANDRA WOOD
Inspired by Arthur Schnitzler's LA RONDE

Cast

Darren Ellis

Gemma Higginbotham

Director	**Natalie Abrahami**
Choreographer	**Ugo Dehaes**
Designer	**Tom Scutt**
Composer	**Tom Mills**
Lighting Designer	**Lee Curran**
Sound Director	**Elena Peña**
Assistant Director	**Sasha Shevtsova**
Production Manager	**Nick Abbott**
Technical Production Assistant	**Joe Schermoly**
Stage Manager	**Bonnie Morris**
Production Electrician	**Chris Porter**
Design Assistants	**Molly Einchcomb** **Verity Sadler**
Musicians	**Hannah Bristow** (Vocals) **Stella Page** (Violin) **James Ryan** (Drums)
Press	**Clióna Roberts for CRPR** cliona@crpr.co.uk | 07754 756504
Rehearsal Photographer	**Bill Knight**
Rehearsal Artist	**Deborah Pearse**

Subsidised rehearsal facilities provided by JERWOOD **SPACE**

Biographies

Nick Abbott
Production Manager

Nick is Production and Technical Manager at the Gate. For the Gate credits include: *State of Emergency*, *Hedda*, *...Sisters*, *Shoot/Get Treasure/Repeat*, *The Internationalist*, *Press*, *I Am Falling* (also Sadler's Wells). Nick was Technical Manager at the Chelsea Theatre for *Sacred* and has worked in the Sound Department on various ballets and operas at the Royal Opera House.

Natalie Abrahami
Director

Natalie is joint Artistic Director of the Gate Theatre. For the Gate credits include: *The Internationalist*, *Women in Love*, *The Car Cemetery*. Other theatre includes: Alexandra Wood's *The Eleventh Capital* (Royal Court); Samuel Beckett's *Play and Not I* (Battersea Arts Centre); Amélie Nothomb's *Human Rites*, Vassily Sigarev's *Plasticine* (Southwark Playhouse). Natalie was awarded the James Menzies-Kitchin Director's Award in 2005.

Lee Curran
Lighting Designer

Lee began his career touring with companies and choreographers including Jonathan Burrows, Mark Baldwin, VTOL, Jeremy James and Michael Clark. Lighting designs at this time included pieces for Burrows, Baldwin and James. Lee is currently Technical Director of the ICA in London, and recent work includes designs for artists such as Probe, Rafael Bonachela and Hofesh Shechter - including the latter's acclaimed *In Your Rooms/Uprising* and *The Perfect Human* (CandoCo).

Ugo Dehaes
Choreographer

Ugo studied dance with David Hernandez, Benoit Lachambre and Saburro Teshigawara and also at PARTS (Anne-Teresa De Keersmaeker). In 1998 Ugo joined Meg Stuart and Damaged Goods for *Appetite* and *Highway 101*. Since 2000 Ugo also worked for Arco Renz, Gisèle Vienne and Etienne Bideau-Rey, Emil Hrvatin, Kataline Patkaï, Nada Gambier and Heine Avdal. His own work includes: *lijfstof* (collaboration with Charlotte Vanden Eynde), *Coupure*, *ROEST*, *Rozenblad*, *Couple-like* (collaboration with Keren Levi) and *FORCES*.

Darren Ellis
Performer

Darren trained at Rambert Dance School (1987-90) and the Laban Centre as part of Transitions Dance Company (1990-91). He has danced with David Massingham Dance, Janet Smith, PAGE Dance Theatre (Frieburg, Germany), Small Bones Dance Company, Jeremy James Company, Matthew Bourne (*Swan Lake* original cast, *Cinderella*, *Nutcracker!* and *Play Without Words)*, Random Dance Company, Mark Bruce Dance Company and Richard Alston Dance Company (Rehearsal Director 2005-07 and dancer 2007-08). As a choreographer Darren has made two pieces for his own company *Romeo Error* and *Good to Go*. He also choreographed for Richard Alston Company (*Tempt My Better Angel* and *No More Ghosts*).

Gemma Higginbotham
Performer

Gemma studied at Northern School of Contemporary Dance, Leeds and PARTS (Performing Arts Research and Training Studios) Brussels, Belgium. Gemma has been based in Belgium since 1998 although her work and collaborations take her all over Europe. Gemma has worked as dancer/performer with Michelle Anne De Mey, Akram Khan, Manuela Rastaldi, Rasmus Ölme, Max Cuccaro, Philippe Blanchard/Adekwhat, Andy Deneys/Galothar, Kris Verdonck/Still Lab and Ugo Dehaes as well as taking part in two films by Theiry De Mey. Her own work includes: *Too Much Night Ego* (2004), *One's Company, Two's A Crowd* (2006) and *Bits Of Bobs Life* (2008).

Tom Mills
Composer

Tom is a musician and composer, and occasionally works with video, filming and producing live shows, online documentaries and blogs. He plays bass guitar, double bass and sings backing vocals in Brighton-based band *Passenger* and works as a session musician. Work as a composer includes: *Edward Gant's Amazing Feats of Loneliness* (Headlong, UK Tour March 2009); *Metropolis* (Theatre Royal, Bath); *Othello* (Assembly Rooms, Bath). As sound designer: *Assassins* (Eyebrow Productions). As an actor/musician: *The Good Person of Szechwan*, *The Berlin* Cabaret (Theatre Royal, Bath). As musical director: *Return to the Forbidden Planet* (Bath Spa Music Society), *Band of Blues Brothers* (Panthelion Productions).

Bonnie Morris
Stage Manager

Bonnie studied Drama at Bristol University and trained in Stage Management and Technical Theatre at LAMDA. She has worked for the Gate since January 2008 having previously stage managed *I Am Falling* (including Sadler's Wells transfer), *Hedda* and *State of Emergency*. Other theatre includes: *Relocated, Bliss, The Eleventh Capital* (Royal Court Theatre); *Faustus, Angels In America* (Headlong Theatre, national tours).

Elena Peña
Sound Designer

For the Gate credits include: *The Internationalist* (Sound Design Assistant). Other sound credits include: *Festival of Firsts, Summer Collection*, Helen Chadwick's *Dalston Songs, Voices Across the World* (Linbury Theatre, Royal Opera House). As Sound Designer: *Building Babble* (Attic People); *Fish Story* (People Can Run); *Punch and Judy Redux* (Dissentertainment); Vassily Sigarev's *Plasticine* (Southwark Playhouse). As Associate Sound Designer: *If That's All There Is* (Inspector Sands Theatre Company, Lyric Hammersmith).

Joe Schermoley
Technical Production Assistant

Joe recently moved to London from Chicago where he studied Set Design & Art History at Northwestern University. Work as a set designer and technician in Chicago theatre includes: *Richard III, The Constant Wife, The Mark of Zorro* and *The Aristocrats*. Joe is very happy to have joined the Gate Theatre for this production of *Unbroken* and plans to continue working in London theatre for the foreseeable future.

Tom Scutt
Designer

For the Gate credits include: *The Internationalist*. Other theatre includes: *Gulliver* (winner of 2007 Linbury Biennial Prize & Jocelyn Herbert Award), *Edward Gant's Amazing Feats of Loneliness* (Headlong); *Bay* (Young Vic); *The Merchant of Venice* (Octagon Theatre – Manchester Evening News award nominated Best Design 2008); *Metropolis* (Theatre Royal Bath); *The Observer* (design consultant, National Theatre Studio); *Paradise Lost* (Southwark Playhouse); *Mad Funny Just* (winner of the 2008 'Old Vic New Voices Award'); *The Water Harvest* (Theatre 503); *Return* (Watford); *The Comedy of Errors* (RSC); *Skellig* (onO Productions); *Loaded* (Fireraisers Theatre); *Branwen* (Wales Millennium Centre); *Dog Tags* (European Live Arts Network).

Sasha Shevtsova
Assistant Director

Sasha trained at The Laban Dance Centre; Trinity College, Cambridge; Sciences Po, Paris and The Moscow Art Theatre School. At Cambridge she choreographed numerous theatre productions. Her theatre work includes, as director and choreographer: an adaptation of Georges Perec's *W* (Battersea Arts Centre). As assistant director: *Richard III – An Arab Tragedy* (dir. Sulayman Al-Bassam, Bouffes du Nord, Paris).

Alexandra Wood
Writer

Alexandra is a graduate of Birmingham University's MPhil(B) Playwriting Studies course. She was a member of the Royal Court Young Writers' Invitation Group and is now a Playwright-in-Residence at the Finborough Theatre. Theatre includes: *miles to go* (Nabokov Theatre, Latitude Festival); *The Lion's Mouth* (Rough Cut at the Royal Court); *The Eleventh Capital* (Royal Court). In 2007 Alexandra was awarded the prestigious George Devine Award.

The Gate would like to thank the following people for their help with this production: Almeida Theatre, AKA, Lady Angela Bernstein, Donmar Warehouse, Carolyn Downing, Eurostar, Gate Bar, Elen Griffiths, Mark Goddard, Patrick Laurie, Rita & Michael Laven, Koron Kossow at The Place, Mary Rendall, Titus Sharpe, Gareth Shelton, Steve Zissler.

Production Image
© Alberto Vajrabukka
www.flickr.com/photos/vajra

GATE

The Gate, London's international theatre in the heart of Notting Hill, is renowned for its inventive use of space and the exceptional artists it attracts. An environment in which artists can create first-class and original theatre, the Gate is a springboard of opportunity, allowing emerging artists to excel and make their mark. With an average audience capacity of seventy, the space has challenged and inspired directors and designers for 30 years, making it famous for being one of the most flexible and transformable spaces in London.

"Great riches in a small space" *Sunday Times*

As joint Artistic Directors, Natalie Abrahami and Carrie Cracknell continue to create international work of the highest standard, which provides audiences with a unique and provocative experience.

**"Under Natalie Abrahami and Carrie Cracknell this 70 seater theatre is
suddenly out there in the vanguard of all that is exciting, explosive and
invigorating in British theatre. It has become a place of possibilities."**
Lyn Gardner, The Guardian

30 YEARS OF EXPLOSIVE INTERNATIONAL THEATRE 1979-2009

Courageous. Adventurous. Indomitable. Risk-taking. Spirited. Seminal. Renowned. All words that have been used to describe our much-loved theatre during the past thirty years.

In 1979 Lou Stein, an American theatrical entrepreneur with visionary ideas and a strong interest in European theatre and politics, applied for the lease of a run down studio over an equally run down ale house in bohemian Notting Hill. The Prince Albert's neighbours were artists, philosophers, writers and bums, perfect company for a burgeoning theatre with radical ideas.

The London Times reflected the Gate's rapidly growing reputation:

"Lou Stein has transformed a room above a public house in Notting Hill into a theatre with a remarkable repertoire. In a space not much larger than a cupboard he has adapted and presented novels, and resurrected plays that have been grossly neglected elsewhere in Britain."

From the very first there was strong local support for the theatre - John Cleese gave the first donation of £10 towards Stein's work. We continue to have an army of loyal local supporters today, some of whom vividly remember the Lou Stein days.

In 1985 Stein handed over the reigns to Giles Croft and in 1990 the Gate became home to an ambitious young director by the name of Stephen Daldry, who cemented its reputation as a place of international tastes and talents. Between 1992 and 2007, the Gate was home to equally visionary artistic directors. Laurence Boswell, David Farr, Mick Gordon, Erica Whyman and Thea Sharrock each made a huge impact on the tiny space. Every one of these artists shared a delight in the freedom to fail and in the lightfootedness that comes with creating first class work on a shoestring. The Gate has won numerous awards and attracted many up-and-coming actors who have cut their teeth here and gone on to glittering careers.

Which brings us to 2009. As a venue which is continuously described as 'reinventing itself', as presenting 'new eras in theatre making' and 'launching careers of influential artists', 2009 will be a year for reflection and also a year for looking forward. A year for ensuring that the work presented by Natalie and Carrie continues in the indomitable spirit for which "London's most courageous theatre" is famous.

JO DANVERS PRODUCER

'THE GATE - STILL SWINGING AFTER 30 YEARS'
SIR TOM STOPPARD

SUPPORT THE **GATE**

We try to ensure that our creative ambitions are not bound by financial pressures; however, we rely on the generosity of our supporters for almost a third of our income in order to continue challenging form and breaking boundaries.

JOIN US! We need supporters who...

- **LOVE COMING TO THE GATE**
- **INTRODUCE THEIR FRIENDS TO THE GATE**
- **GIVE GENEROUSLY TO HELP THE GATE**

Supporters of the Gate receive benefits such as invitations to a host of events, including exclusive post-show drinks with casts and creative teams, a backstage glimpse of the running of the theatre, regular newsletters and priority booking. Supporters also have the opportunity to develop a close relationship with the Gate Theatre and the team who run it.

The very nature of our tiny venue means that you can see just how significant the support you give is - to our work, to the nurturing of emerging talent and in bringing international theatre to London.

For more information on the Gate's work and how to support it, please visit www.gatetheatre.co.uk or contact Sam Sargant on 020 7229 5387 or sam@gatetheatre.co.uk.

The Gate would like to thank the following for their continued generous support:

Gate Guardians Emma and Mike Davies, Edward Field, Miles Morland, Jon and NoraLee Sedmak, Hilary and Stuart Williams, Anda and Bill Winters

Gate Keepers Russ and Linda Carr, Lauren Clancy, Robert Devereux and Vanessa Branson, Cory Edelman Moss, David and Alexandra Emmerson, Leslie Feeney, Eric Fellner, Nick Ferguson, Marianne Hinton, Tony Mackintosh, Oberon Books, Elizabeth Price, David and Susie Sainsbury, The Ulrich Family

Gate Lovers Ariane Braillard, Kay Ellen Consolver and John Storkerson, Charles Cormick, James Fleming, Joachim Fleury, Bill and Stephanie Knight, David and Linda Lakhdhir, David Pike, Kerri Ratcliffe, Maurits Schouten, Kathryn Smith and Ike Udechuku, Sir Tom Stoppard

Special thanks to Jenny Hall

Trusts & Foundations Anonymous, Arts Council England, Earls Court & Olympia Charitable Trust, The Eranda Foundation, Jerwood Charitable Foundation, The Mercers' Company, OAK Foundation, The Prince's Foundation for Children & the Arts, Royal Borough of Kensington & Chelsea.

PARTICIPATE AT THE **GATE**

The Gate Theatre has recently launched a new and exciting participation initiative. We are creating projects with local residents and forming relationships across London.

The Gate is located in the Royal Borough of Kensington and Chelsea, one of the most ethnically and economically diverse in Britain. More than one hundred different languages are spoken in our Borough. This represents a wealth of experience, perspectives and stories that we are keen to engage with, finding connections between our international repertoire and our multicultural community.

The Gate's Participation Projects are aimed at discovering who our community is, connecting with local people of all ages both within our Borough and across London.

Visit our website at www.gatetheatre.co.uk or contact Lu Kemp on 020 7229 5387 or lu@gatetheatre.co.uk to get involved with our exciting projects.

UP...UP...AND A PLAY!

Local residents and friends of the Gate have taken photographs of red balloons in our Borough, and further afield.

We are exhibiting these images, the beautiful and the bizarre, in the Gate Theatre foyer throughout the run of *Unbroken*.

Take a moment to have a look through the collection of images displayed in the theatre foyer or to see a larger collection of the images collected visit:

http://www.flickr.com/photos/33168573@N02/show/

NEXT AT THE **GATE**

THE **GATE** ELSEWHERE

UNBROKEN

Alexandra Wood

Inspired by Schnitzler's

La Ronde

For Gugs and Grandbear

Characters

AMY
JOHNNO
LAURA
STEVE
ZOE
DAVID

A forward slash in the text (/) marks the point where the next speaker interrupts.

Author's Note

There are some differences between the published text and that used in the first production of the play. The director, Natalie Abrahami, created a dance theatre piece for which some of the dialogue here was cut in the interests of economy.

A.W.

I

The green room backstage at a gig.

Throughout the scene, JOHNNO *and* AMY *don't take their eyes off one another.*

JOHNNO. I know it sounds like a line, but I saw you from the stage, I did. We made eye contact. Threw me. And then you were with Lydia backstage and I knew we were destined to meet.

AMY. Yeah, that does sound like a line.

JOHNNO. But you did, didn't you. You caught my eye in the middle of Broken. Had to play the chorus again coz I lost my place for a minute.

AMY. Thought it was part of it.

JOHNNO. Well that's coz I'm a professional isn't it.

Pause.

AMY. It was good. The gig.

JOHNNO. Please. Stop. Such praise.

AMY. I mean, actually it's not really my kind of music, so

JOHNNO. Then why did you come?

AMY. Lydia. She's always trying to get me to these things. Thinks it's good for me, open my eyes or something.

JOHNNO. Such beautiful eyes.

AMY. You're kidding right?

JOHNNO *smiles.*

JOHNNO. Yeah.

They're pretty mediocre actually.

AMY. So are yours.

JOHNNO. Well I'm glad we sorted that out.

Pause.

You don't look like sisters.

AMY. Well she's quite a few years younger so

JOHNNO. I thought she was your mother.

AMY *laughs*.

AMY. Seriously, does this stuff ever work?

She smiles.

Pause.

JOHNNO. What does Lydia think you need to open your mediocre eyes to then?

AMY. The fun and crazy world of excess and debauchery I suppose.

JOHNNO. Why? Is your world too boring?

AMY. In Lydia's eyes, undoubtedly, yes.

JOHNNO. What world's that then?

AMY. You know, marriage.

Pause.

Nine-to-five. Mortgage. That kind of thing.

Pause.

Who am I kidding, she's right. That's why I come to these things, even when I don't like the music.

JOHNNO. A moment ago it was good.

AMY. Well a moment ago my eyes were beautiful, now they're mediocre. Things change.

JOHNNO. Do you know who I am?

AMY *laughs*.

No, not in a do you know who I am way but as in, do you even know what the band's called?

AMY. Encore or something?

JOHNNO *laughs*.

JOHNNO. Close enough.

AMY. My husband, David, he likes you.

JOHNNO. Perhaps he should've come instead.

AMY. He's got work.

Pause.

JOHNNO. My girlfriend's the same. Always working.

AMY. What's she do?

JOHNNO. She's Tasha Hart.

AMY. And that's what she does is it?

JOHNNO *smiles*.

JOHNNO. Well, yes actually. Pretty much.

AMY. And that's demanding?

JOHNNO. She takes it very seriously.

AMY. The job or herself?

JOHNNO. They're kind of the same thing.

AMY. So when she's with you she's working?

JOHNNO. Well I don't like to think she is, but, maybe.

AMY. I think David feels like he is. When he's with me.

Pause.

JOHNNO. Yeah you seem like pretty hard work.

AMY. He doesn't love me.

Silence.

I don't think he's ever looked at me like you are. Even when we first met.

Pause.

JOHNNO. I can stop if

AMY. No.

JOHNNO. Good, I didn't really want to.

Tasha's always wearing sunglasses so I never know where she's looking. But it's probably not at me.

AMY. Yeah I bet you're really starved of attention. I mean there were only, how many thousands of women in the audience tonight looking at you?

JOHNNO. Didn't notice them. I only saw you.

AMY *smiles.*

Silence.

AMY. Well, this should get Lydia off my back for a while.

JOHNNO. What should?

AMY. Me nattering to a real live rockstar.

JOHNNO *smiles.*

JOHNNO. Nattering?

AMY. Yes, nattering.

JOHNNO. Is that what we're doing?

AMY. Yes.

JOHNNO. Doesn't sound very rock'n'roll.

Pause.

I can show you some excess and debauchery if you'd like.

AMY. I think I should go.

JOHNNO. No, don't. Lydia would want you to stay.

AMY. And Tasha?

JOHNNO. Tasha? Why would she mind? We're just nattering.

AMY. Well I think David would so

JOHNNO. Really? It doesn't sound like he would.

Pause.

Come on. Natter with me some more.

AMY. Stop looking at me like that.

JOHNNO. Like what?

Pause.

AMY. I'd better let you go.

JOHNNO. You'll let me go? That's very kind, but I'm perfectly happy here.

AMY. I'm sure you have some minions that need you to shout at them or something.

He stares at her intensely. Without taking her eyes off him, she starts to back away.

JOHNNO. I'm enjoying our natter Amy, don't go.

She continues to back away.

(*Louder.*) I saw you from the stage, amongst a crowd of thousands, so go to the other side of the room if you like, I'll still see you.

She moves towards him again to quieten him.

AMY. Shhhh.

She goes to put her finger on his mouth but pulls away at the last second.

Pause.

JOHNNO. What are you shushing me for? We're just having a natter.

AMY. There's no need to shout, that's all.

JOHNNO. That wasn't shouting.

AMY. Just shhhh.

JOHNNO. You can't walk away can you? Because you're
scared no one will ever look at you like this again.

Pause.

AMY *turns, breaking the gaze for the first time.*

What are you proving by walking away?

Pause.

You don't get a prize for sticking at it Amy. You don't win
anything.

He turns her to face him.

*He takes her hand, and without breaking their gaze, leads
her over to a private alcove.*

I saw you from the stage. It threw me.

*He kisses her. He pulls away to say something but she kisses
him before he can. The kissing grows more passionate and
they have sex right there.*

AMY *and* JOHNNO *continue to hold each other's gaze.*
AMY *is laughing.*

JOHNNO *smiles.*

She can't stop.

II

A cramped living room in LAURA *and* STEVE*'s terraced house.*

JOHNNO *is on the sofa.*

LAURA. Still white three sugars?

JOHNNO. Actually, I've cut down to two now.

LAURA. Two sugars? John Wilson, it's like I don't know who you are any more.

She goes to the kitchen to make the tea.

JOHNNO. You know, gotta keep in shape.

LAURA (*from the kitchen*). Yeah well, those jeans don't leave much to the imagination do they. Tighter than mine.

JOHNNO *stands and starts examining some of the ornaments.*

Put some music on if you want. Prob'ly got some of yours there actually.

JOHNNO. Nah, it's okay.

LAURA. Don't judge me. Most of it's Steve's.

Silence.

JOHNNO *looks through the CD collection.*

JOHNNO. How's Steve?

LAURA. Okay.

Silence.

Hey, we should go down Mr Patel's and see how long it takes for a mob to form around you.

JOHNNO. He still there?

LAURA. Mainly Sanjay runs things now, but yeah, he still sits behind the counter guarding the penny sweets.

JOHNNO. Suspicious bastard.

LAURA. Be fair. Least he never asked for ID.

JOHNNO. I was ID'd the other day at Tesco, buying a lighter for one of the lads, wasn't even for me.

LAURA. You shop at Tesco?

Pause.

Never could get served. Babyface.

JOHNNO. Didn't have any on me, but they were selling *Heat* at the counter and I said, look, I don't mean to be, you know, but I'm in that magazine there, look, and I showed her and she just said, doesn't say how old you are though, does it. And I said, look, I'm pictured coming out of a club, where they sell alcohol, and she said, you look like a sweet enough lad but this is my job on the line, if you're underage I'm the one has to pay the penalty, so I'm sorry but I can't do it.

LAURA. Yeah, they do, my mate Kirstie works there and they're really strict with 'em.

JOHNNO. And as I was leaving this girl ran up behind me, now she looked underage, and gave me a lighter, she'd just bought it. She'd written her mobile number on it.

Pause.

LAURA. Rung her yet?

JOHNNO. I just said, she looked about twelve.

LAURA. Well I don't know John.

Silence.

Who you shagging at the moment then?

Pause.

Or don't you kiss and tell now?

JOHNNO. I've never done that. When did I do that?

LAURA. All right.

JOHNNO. No, you said it like I'd done it to you or something.

LAURA. Just teasing John.

Silence.

LAURA *enters the living room with two mugs of tea.*
JOHNNO *is still looking at the CD collection. She hands*
JOHNNO *his tea.*

Like I said, don't judge me, Steve's got no taste.

JOHNNO. I don't know, I reckon he's done pretty well for
himself.

LAURA *smiles.*

LAURA. What about you?

Unbelievable.

JOHNNO. Yeah, done all right.

LAURA. I knew you would.

JOHNNO. Did you though? Did you ever actually think I'd
make it?

LAURA. Course.

Pause.

Anyone that wants something that much'll get it.

JOHNNO. Not just about wanting it.

LAURA. No but

JOHNNO. Lots of things I want that I can't get.

Pause.

LAURA. Don't believe that John. Not going to get me to feel
sorry for you, don't buy it, sorry.

JOHNNO. It's true.

LAURA. Name one.

JOHNNO *sips his tea.*

JOHNNO. This is nice, thanks.

LAURA. Well, I can make tea.

Pause.

JOHNNO. You working?

LAURA. Was doing a bit of reception work but company down-sized so

S'all right though, me and Steve was thinking about starting a family anyway.

JOHNNO. Thought you'd 'ave a couple by now.

Silence.

But plenty of time. Think it'd be nice to have kids while you're young enough to enjoy 'em though.

LAURA. Think about 'aving kids a lot do you?

JOHNNO. Just recently.

Prob'ly just the whole new year thing. Makes you reassess and all that.

Pause.

LAURA. Are you broody? Is John Wilson broody? No way.

JOHNNO. I'm not.

LAURA. You are, you're blushing.

JOHNNO. Just thought about it Laura, that's all.

Pause.

LAURA. You always said you'd never want kids.

JOHNNO *shrugs.*

Silence.

Read you're shagging that Tasha Hart.

JOHNNO. Our publicist arranged a few dates.

LAURA. How romantic.

JOHNNO. Haven't seen her in a couple of months, so

LAURA. She's pretty.

Pause.

JOHNNO. Laura, have you heard my song, Broken?

LAURA. Listened to all your songs, so 'spect so.

JOHNNO. It's on the Silver Cord / album.

LAURA. Course I have.

JOIINNO. Right.

Silence.

LAURA. That it?

JOHNNO. It's about you.

LAURA *nods.*

LAURA. Steve always says it is. Tells all his mates.

JOHNNO. Well he's right.

LAURA *nods.*

Just thought I'd tell you.

LAURA. It's beautiful.

JOHNNO. Do you, really?

LAURA *nods.*

Thanks.

Well, you crushed me Laura. You actually crushed me, but it gave me a lot of material. I think that if you hadn't I might never have made it. I sometimes wonder if I could've had the choice, between making it, and keeping you, I sometimes torture myself with it.

LAURA. No point torturing yourself.

JOHNNO. I know.

LAURA. What you got to regret? I'm the one dumped you, the big megastar, how stupid do I look?

Pause.

And I still loved you an' all.

Pause.

No point telling you that now though, look like a right gold-digger.

She laughs.

Silence.

JOHNNO. Why'd you do it then?

LAURA. No point John. There isn't any point in this.

JOHNNO. Yes there is. We could be happy.

JOHNNO *kisses* LAURA.

LAURA. What're you doing? I'm with Steve, and you, you're you aren't you.

JOHNNO *kisses her again. She pulls away.*

John

JOHNNO. What?

LAURA. This is crazy.

JOHNNO. You just said you still love me.

LAURA. Loved you, John, past tense, I don't even know you any more.

JOHNNO. I wrote that song for you.

LAURA. Thank you, it's beautiful, but that doesn't mean

What did you think that meant? Keep me sweet by writing me a song, come running back when Tasha Hart's out of town and you decide you want babies. Have all the celebs got 'em, do you feel out of it? Is that it? Because you never wanted 'em before, you never did, you always said you'd never want them.

JOHNNO. So, I've changed my mind Laura. It's allowed.

JOHNNO *kisses her again. She pushes him off.*

LAURA. John, stop it, okay.

It's been nice seeing you, trip down memory lane, real celebrity in my front room, but

Steve could be back any moment, took the afternoon off.

JOHNNO. I'd choose you Laura.

LAURA. I told you that was pointless.

JOHNNO. I know you still love me. You dumped me because you thought we wanted different things, not because you didn't love me.

JOHNNO *holds* LAURA *firmly.*

LAURA. John, please, we do want different things.

I do love you, of course I do, but I'm with Steve.

JOHNNO. You're just scared.

LAURA. I am Johnno, yes, I am.

JOHNNO. It's all right to feel scared.

JOHNNO *kisses her.*

LAURA. I know, we've got history, but let's not ruin it.

JOHNNO. I'm hard Laura, I'm always hard for you.

LAURA. Please John.

JOHNNO *unzips his jeans then pushes up* LAURA*'s skirt.*

John no, Steve'll be back any minute.

JOHNNO. Shhh.

JOHNNO *starts to finger* LAURA.

See you're wet.

LAURA. I'm not John, I'm scared.

JOHNNO. Shhh. We can be like we were.

LAURA. We can't John.

JOHNNO. Don't you want to be?

JOHNNO *fucks* LAURA. *She doesn't make a sound.*

Silence.

He kisses her. LAURA *gets up abruptly.*

What's wrong?

LAURA *paces.*

Laura?

LAURA. What's wrong?

She laughs.

Get out. Now.

JOHNNO. Laura.

LAURA. I'll call the police, do you want that?

JOHNNO. The police?

LAURA. Yeah, that wouldn't look good for you, would it?

I'm counting to five. If you're not out / by then

JOHNNO. Laura, calm down, okay.

I know you must feel bad about Steve but

LAURA. Feel bad? It was hardly adultery.

Pause.

JOHNNO. What's that mean?

LAURA. Fuck off.

JOHNNO. Laura, I'll go if you want me to, of course I will. I'd never do anything you didn't want.

Pause.

LAURA. Get out then.

JOHNNO. I miss you.

Pause.

LAURA. Five. Four. Three. / Two. One.

JOHNNO. I do. Laura? I do miss you. I want you back.

Silence.

LAURA *opens the front door and stands by it.*

Pause.

JOHNNO *leaves.*

III

That evening. LAURA *and* STEVE*'s bedroom. It's late.*

LAURA*'s in bed, she's been waiting.* STEVE *is undressing in silence.*

LAURA. Thought you might've been back earlier.

STEVE. Went for a drink with the lads.

Pause.

LAURA. Just thought you might come back straight after, that's all.

STEVE. Yeah, sorry.

LAURA. Hoped I guess.

STEVE. Just needed some time, Laura, I'm sorry.

LAURA. Not having a go Steve. Not saying hoped to make you feel bad. Hoped in that, well, if it was good news you would've come straight back here to tell me, wouldn't you. Just really wanted to see you come through the door this afternoon.

But you didn't. And it wasn't good news, was it?

Pause.

STEVE. No.

LAURA *nods.*

LAURA. Been sitting here working out the odds and figured it couldn't be or you would've come straight back here to make love to me, wouldn't you?

Pause.

STEVE. She said it's me, like we suspected.

Pause.

I'm really sorry Laura.

Pause.

LAURA. No, it's

STEVE. At least now we know what the problem's been and we can

Well, I mean, there are options.

LAURA *nods.*

There's always adop/tion, and I

LAURA I want my own children.

STEVE. I know, and I promise, we'll do everything we can, it doesn't matter about the cost.

LAURA. There's really no chance?

STEVE. The odds are against it Laura.

LAURA. Okay, fine, but how against it?

STEVE. Nought point five per cent chance, it's really not good.

LAURA. So there is still a chance?

STEVE. Not one worth pinning your hopes on.

Silence.

LAURA. Do you know how long I've wanted kids?

STEVE. I know.

LAURA. Do you know what I've given up to have them?

STEVE. Given up? What d'you mean given up? True love, is that what you mean? / A pool and wardrobes full of designer dresses you've only worn once?

LAURA. No, just different paths I could've

STEVE (*continuing*). Is that what you mean? / Well I'm sorry to waste your time

LAURA. Choices I've made, Steve, just that choices I've made, they've always been based on knowing that more than anything, I want to be a mother. That's dictated / most of the decisions

STEVE. I'm going to do everything I can to help you, us have children, okay? I promise. We have options, there are lots of options. And who knows, maybe you're right, nought point five is still a chance, isn't it, so this is a setback Laura, but it's in no way the end.

Pause.

It's not the end. Is it?

Pause.

Because actually Laura this is hardly great news for me. It's not easy to learn that your boys are pretty fucking lazy, practically fucking comatose in fact. And I've always considered myself dad material. We'd be a great team, you've always said that, haven't you? Because there are loads of men out there who might be able to father a kid, but they'd be shit dads. Aren't there? Loads of selfish, career-obsessed, abusive maybe, men who'd be shit dads. Kids themselves. But I'd be a good dad. You know that. I would, wouldn't I?

LAURA. Yes.

STEVE. You've always said it.

LAURA. I know, because it's true.

STEVE. Okay. So this isn't the end then.

Pause.

STEVE *goes over to* LAURA.

We'll find a way.

Won't we?

LAURA *holds* STEVE. *He puts his arms around her.*

LAURA. I wish you'd let me go with you.

She kisses him. He gratefully kisses her back. They fall into their familiar routine and have sex the way they normally do, but with a renewed sense of urgency.

They lie back together.

Nought point five is still a chance, isn't it.

STEVE. Sure.

Pause.

I'm sorry I didn't come straight back after. I should've.

LAURA. It's fine.

STEVE. What did you get up to?

IV

A speed-dating event.

ZOE *sits at a small table.* STEVE *sits down opposite her.*

ZOE. Hi, I'm Zoe.

STEVE. Steve.

ZOE. So, you here for a friend?

STEVE. Yeah, Will.

ZOE. Which one's Will then?

STEVE. You just spoke to him.

ZOE. Oh, right. Let me guess, you're doing him a favour,
    coming along with him.

STEVE. Yeah, I am actually. He's writing an article on speed-
    dating, so

ZOE. Funny, he said you were writing the article.

STEVE. Did he?

   Pause.

   You here with a friend too then?

ZOE. No.

STEVE. Oh. Right.

   Pause.

ZOE. S'okay. Don't need to feel sorry for me. I do have friends.
    Just not single ones.

   Came here to meet some.

STEVE. Friends?

ZOE. Yes.

STEVE smiles.

Pause.

So, what do you do Steve?

Pause.

Sorry, I know it's a clichéd question, but it's not a hard one, is it?

STEVE. No, it's just you're quite

ZOE. You've already formed an opinion have you?

STEVE. Not really, I was just going to say I don't know actually.

ZOE. I'm quite, you don't know.

STEVE. Yes.

ZOE smiles.

ZOE. I'll take that.

STEVE. Thanks.

I'm a personal trainer.

ZOE. I thought you probably did something physical. You've got the body.

STEVE. What? These old things.

He flexes a bicep. ZOE feels it.

That's six days a week down the gym right there.

ZOE. Impressive. I like a man to look good.

STEVE drops his arm.

STEVE. Is that on your checklist?

ZOE. I don't have a checklist.

STEVE. It's just that you seem like you could.

ZOE (*indicating pen and paper in her hand*). This is just so I don't forget who I've met. They gave it to me, I wouldn't normally go out with a scorecard in my bag.

STEVE. It's a scorecard?

ZOE. Not exactly, I don't know what they call it.

Aren't you filling one out?

STEVE. No.

ZOE. Oh that's right, you don't need to take down notes, coz this is just a thing you're doing for Will. Coz you're a good mate.

STEVE. I reckon if someone's worth remembering, I won't need a scorecard.

ZOE *makes a note.*

What did you write?

ZOE. Good memory. Useful gene.

Pause.

It was a joke Steve. Do I look like some baby-crazy psycho woman?

Look, I didn't write anything. I just scribbled.

She shows him her scorecard.

See.

He looks at it.

I don't think I need to make a note on you.

Pause.

STEVE. You think Will's a potentially embarrassing drunk?

STEVE *laughs.*

ZOE. You weren't supposed to read my notes.

STEVE. He is a pretty embarrassing drunk actually. Never get him to make a speech at your wedding, I'm warning you.

Pause.

ZOE. Are you married?

Pause.

STEVE. Yeah, I am.

ZOE. But you're not wearing a wedding ring.

Pause.

STEVE. Didn't think they'd let me in if I was wearing one.

ZOE. Clever.

STEVE. I'm just being honest Zoe, I'm sorry.

Pause.

ZOE. I need a date.

STEVE. Well you've come to the right place.

ZOE. Except the only guy I've liked so far is married.

Pause.

Does your wife know you're here?

STEVE. Yes.

ZOE. Liar.

STEVE. She does.

ZOE. Okay, so then if she doesn't mind you coming here and having like ten dates, she won't mind if you take me on one more.

STEVE. Um

ZOE. And it's not even a proper date. It's this work thing. Black tie. I really need to go, all the partners will be there, but I can't turn up on my own.

STEVE. You came here on your own.

ZOE. Okay, well maybe I just don't want to turn up on my own.

Pause.

STEVE. Will's a nice guy. And he's not that embarrassing, it's really only champagne that does / that to him.

ZOE. I don't like Will.

Pause.

It's just a work thing. The least romantic night out in the world, I promise you. If she let you come to this then

STEVE. Are you in sales or something?

ZOE. I came here looking for a date Steve. In a way, you being married, that's the best possible option, it'll be simpler. I'll be able to concentrate on networking without worrying. And you know, there'll be lots of people there with money to burn, lots of people who might like a personal trainer.

STEVE. So it's a business proposition?

ZOE. Pretty much, yes.

STEVE. I could do with some more clients. We're trying for a baby.

ZOE. A baby? Well then you're going to need as much cash as possible.

Pause.

STEVE. Okay, look, fuck it, I'm sure she'll be fine with it. It's business right?

ZOE. Sure. So I'll give you my number and give me a call in the next few days.

STEVE. Cool.

ZOE. Okay, it's 07700 900 462. Do you want to borrow my pen?

STEVE. No, it's fine, I'll remember it.

The sound of the bell ringing. STEVE stands and moves on to the next 'date'.

Scene V

Early on a Friday evening. In the office.

DAVID *is at his desk, trying to work.* ZOE *stands in the doorway, holding out some cake, wrapped in a party napkin.*

ZOE. It's Kate's. It's her birthday. There was cake.

DAVID. Who's Kate?

ZOE. Kate. Mark's assistant.

DAVID *still doesn't know her.*

The pretty one. Long dark hair, always wears pencil skirt suits. Everyone knows who she is David.

DAVID. I'll take your word for it.

Pause.

ZOE *offers* DAVID *the cake.*

Thanks but I'm not hungry.

ZOE. Sure?

DAVID *nods.*

Brilliant. (*She eats the cake.*) It's really good but they were well stingy slices.

Pause.

You staying here all night then?

DAVID. I'm staying until I've finished my work.

ZOE. You're dedicated. I like that. It's good to have a boss who doesn't just dump all the work on his underlings.

DAVID. I'm glad you approve Zoe.

ZOE. Yeah, and our meagre opinions matter to you, I like that too.

She smiles.

Pause. DAVID *attempts to get back to work.*

You excited about the weekend? The big wedding.

DAVID. Yeah, it should be good.

ZOE. Shouldn't you be out getting Joe drunk or something?

DAVID. We had the stag last weekend.

ZOE. Still.

DAVID. Liz didn't want him drunk the night before.

ZOE. Got her claws in that one hasn't she.

What's she like, Liz? Can't imagine the type of woman that'd tie Joe down.

Pause.

DAVID. Zoe, I'm actually pretty busy, as you say, big weekend ahead, need to get this done so

ZOE. I could help.

DAVID. No, I don't think so.

ZOE. What is it? The Lawson report? I've been working on that, I could help.

DAVID. No. Thanks.

ZOE *goes to the computer to see what he's working on.*
DAVID *stands up to block her view. She takes a step back.*

ZOE. Best-man-speech material? You haven't written it yet?

DAVID. That's what I'm trying to do now Zoe.

ZOE. Oh let me help, / I'm really good at this stuff.

DAVID. I'm fine.

ZOE (*continuing*). You can't use generic anecdotes from some lame website for your best mate's wedding. I can't let you do that.

DAVID. I won't hold you personally responsible Zoe, / don't worry.

ZOE. I'm good at presenting though, aren't I?

DAVID. Yes, you are.

ZOE. D'you think?

She smiles.

So let me help.

DAVID. This is a bit different.

ZOE. Look, just tell me what you've got so far and we can go from there.

DAVID *picks up one of the pieces of paper he was working on. He reluctantly reads it out.*

DAVID. Good evening ladies and gentlemen. I must admit to being rather nervous about today's speech.

ZOE. Okay, not the most confident start, but go on.

DAVID. As it's a family occasion, I don't want to cause offence by talking in too much detail about Joe's colourful past and have edited out anything that might upset anyone present. So thank you very much, ladies and gentlemen, and goodnight.

ZOE. That's from one of those lame websites isn't it.

DAVID. I didn't ask for your help Zoe.

ZOE. Yeah, but I'm good at this. You need to make it more personal.

DAVID. I think it's best to keep it short and sweet.

ZOE. Yeah, but that's ridiculous.

DAVID. I've got others. (*He picks up another sheet and reads over it.*) Um, when Joe told me he was getting married and he asked me to be his best man

When he asked me

ZOE. Yeah.

DAVID. When he asked me, my world kind of shifted.

Pause.

ZOE. What, coz like you were amazed he was settling down?

DAVID. Yeah.

ZOE. It sounds a bit weird. This is Joe, / there's got to be a million anecdotes you could come up with.

DAVID. I know this is Joe.

ZOE. Just think of a time he's embarrassed himself and share it.

DAVID. I can't think of the right example, the right tone.

ZOE. What else have you got?

ZOE *tries to pick up one of the other sheets but* DAVID *blocks her way.*

DAVID. You can't walk into my office Zoe and start looking through my papers. I could have you fired for that.

ZOE. Fired?

DAVID. I could have confidential papers on my desk, you've no right to

ZOE. Confidential?

DAVID. The point is, you can't come in and

ZOE. I was only trying to help you.

Pause.

DAVID. I appreciate that, thank you Zoe, but it's Friday night, you go and have fun. Isn't Kath having birthday drinks or

ZOE. Kate.

DAVID. Right well go and get drunk at Kate's then. Say happy
birthday to her for me.

ZOE. But you don't even know who she is.

DAVID. No, you're right, but apparently I should, so pass on
my congratulations just in case.

ZOE. You really don't know her?

DAVID. Zoe

Pause.

ZOE. Some of the guys, when you weren't at her cake thing,
they were betting that you didn't even know who she was.
They thought you probably hadn't even noticed her.

Pause.

They were saying you hadn't even noticed her because you
don't really like women.

Silence.

DAVID. That's male banter Zoe. If you don't rub your groin
against every girl at the photocopier you're gay. It's just
banter.

ZOE. I know.

DAVID. I liked Amy enough to marry her.

ZOE. I know. That's what I told them. You're married.

DAVID. Okay.

Pause.

ZOE. Surely you can think of some drunken thing Joe's done
that no one knows about. You're best mates right? You must
have loads of dirt on him.

Pause.

DAVID. This Kate girl. She the sourpuss who walks round the office like the world's about to end?

ZOE. I think she's going for mysterious and enigmatic actually, but yeah. See, you do know who she is.

DAVID. She's not half as pretty as she thinks she is.

ZOE *smiles*.

I like a woman who smiles now and again.

ZOE *smiles*.

Like you, Zoe, you smile a lot. I like that. You've got a lovely smile.

ZOE *smiles*.

ZOE. Didn't think you'd noticed.

DAVID. I'm not blind.

I'm sorry I've been a bit touchy, it's not you, it's, I've got a lot of things on my mind at the moment.

ZOE. The wedding?

DAVID. No, not the wedding, generally, work and

ZOE. Amy?

Pause.

DAVID. But having you around, (*He moves closer.*) it helps.

ZOE. Perhaps I can help relax you.

Pause.

She kisses him. He pulls away.

Does that help?

DAVID *kisses* ZOE. *The kissing becomes more intense but not necessarily passionate.*

I wasn't sure.

DAVID. About what?

ZOE. If you liked me.

DAVID *kisses* ZOE.

DAVID. I like you.

ZOE. And when the guys were say/ing that you

DAVID. They're arseholes.

DAVID *kisses* ZOE.

I really like you Zoe, okay?

He pulls up her skirt and she unzips his trousers. They pause momentarily, then launch themselves into it again. They have fumbled, passionless sex against the desk. It's formulaic and unimaginative.

Afterwards, DAVID *moves away, zipping up his flies.* ZOE *smoothes down her clothing.*

ZOE. You don't have to worry David, I won't tell anyone.

DAVID. I wouldn't ask you to lie.

ZOE. Still, I won't.

Pause.

I like you.

VI

Sunday morning. The open-plan living room/kitchen of DAVID *and* AMY*'s ground-floor flat.*

AMY *is busy making breakfast. The radio is playing. She has her back to the door and doesn't notice* DAVID *when he comes in. He watches her without saying anything for a while. He takes in the room.* AMY *senses him and turns her head.*

AMY. Oh. Morning.

DAVID. You're up early.

AMY. Drunk too much yesterday.

D'you want coffee?

Pause.

David. Coffee?

DAVID *comes up behind her and starts to kiss her neck.*

I was going to do a fry-up anyway, you don't have to

He turns her to face him.

Pause.

He kisses her tenderly on the lips.

Where did that come from?

She kisses him back.

The kissing becomes more passionate and leads on to sex. It is tender and loving.

Afterwards, DAVID *doesn't want to let go.*

David, can I just

DAVID. Just let me, please, for a minute.

He continues holding her. After a while he lets her go.

She rearranges her clothing and puts the kettle on.

AMY. Can't remember the last time we did it in the morning.

Pause.

We should go to more weddings. Think they're good for you.

DAVID. I hate weddings.

AMY. Well obviously something agreed with you.

Coffee darling?

Pause.

DAVID. No.

Pause.

Amy, I had sex with the intern.

Pause.

AMY. I'm sorry?

DAVID. I can't say it was in a bar and some slag was all over me and I was so drunk I didn't know what I was doing, because I did. In my office, on Friday. I was stone-cold sober and I knew what I was doing.

AMY. You just kissed me like you meant it.

She spits.

Pause.

DAVID. I think it's a sign, a sign that things aren't right between us, and I don't want to stay and mess you around, I don't want to lie to you, I won't do that, so I'm leaving. I want out. I hate weddings and I hate marriage. I want a divorce.

Pause.

AMY. Do you hate me?

DAVID. No. I love you.

AMY *laughs*.

I do.

AMY. You don't know what love is.

DAVID. I do know what love is.

Pause.

AMY. I know you do David. But if you think this is love, that it's love to fuck some careerist twelve-year-old and then dare to kiss me like you mean it then

Pause.

It's love to fuck me before telling me you're leaving? You selfish prick. Is that love?

Pause.

Is it?

DAVID. I love you but not as a husband.

AMY. You don't love me.

DAVID. Don't say that / I do.

AMY. Don't you dare tell me what to say and not say.

Silence.

Since when? Since when David have you loved me but not as a husband? Since our first kiss? Since our wedding? Since before you knew me?

DAVID. I don't know.

AMY. Of course you know. Think David.

DAVID. I didn't want this to be

AMY. What?

DAVID. I don't know, bitter, I suppose.

There's no need for it to be

I want to remember us fondly.

AMY. Fondly?

She laughs.

I'm sorry is this not going how you planned? What do you want me to say? Did you expect me to hold you and tell you it's okay, I understand. Because I do understand, David, I do, and I've always known this was coming, it's pretty bloody ironic you do this the day after Joe gets married, I don't know what you imagine can happen between the two of you now, / but you're more deluded than I thought if you think I'm going to hold you and tell you it's okay.

DAVID. What's that supposed to mean?

AMY (*continuing*). You know exactly what it means.

Pause.

I was just thinking, as you were holding me in your arms all of two seconds ago, I was just thinking, he's never looked at me like this. He's never kissed me like this. Something's changed. And do you know what I thought it was, stupid cow, do you know? I thought, maybe the wedding, maybe that's put an end to it, maybe, some sort of closure or

Pause.

But actually, it was us. It put an end to us.

DAVID. Joe's wedding's got nothing to do with this.

AMY. Okay.

DAVID. I had sex with Zoe.

AMY. Oh, so it's Zoe you love is it? It's Zoe, not Joe, who you share some deep connection with is it?

Pause.

DAVID. I think it's a / sign

AMY. Yes, a sign, you said. I think it's an excuse. A convenient shag to get you out of this poor excuse for a marriage.

Silence.

DAVID. So I'm going to my dad's for now.

> And obviously there's a lot to, lawyers and, and I'll pick up my stuff as soon as I can.

AMY. All sorted then.

DAVID. I don't want this to be bitter Amy. I really don't want us to be like those people who get so angry they can't even be in a room together.

AMY. Why? Because you love me?

DAVID. Yes.

AMY. You don't love me David, that's clear. I would've hoped at least you could be honest with me, just for once confide in me, like I was someone you could trust, someone you lived with for five years, someone you were fond of even, but even that was optimistic.

> *Pause.*

DAVID. I'm sorry.

AMY. You're not, you're relieved. I'm willing to believe that whatever sordid little fantasy you acted out over the photocopier meant nothing, in fact I'm pretty sure it did, so don't tell me this is about Zoe, that it's some sort of sign.

> What the hell does that even mean, it's a sign? Yeah, a sign of your lack of imagination. The intern for God's sake David.

> You kissed me like everything was going to be all right.

> *Pause.*

DAVID. It will be.

AMY. You kissed me like you wanted me.

DAVID. I'm sorry.

AMY. If you loved me you wouldn't have done that.

> You don't love me.

Pause.

DAVID. I do.

AMY. Prove it.

Pause.

Kiss me.

Pause.

DAVID. I don't think

I don't think it's appropriate.

AMY. Appropriate? Do you think fucking me just then was appropriate?

DAVID. I'd feel

AMY. Used?

DAVID. No.

AMY. Stupid?

DAVID. No.

AMY. Just me then, / is it.

DAVID. I don't see how kissing you proves I love you. I've already told you, I don't love you in that way, / but that doesn't

AMY. You managed a couple of minutes ago.

DAVID. I wanted our last time / to be something

AMY. I didn't know it was our last time.

DAVID. If you'd known, it would've been different.

AMY. Yeah very different, it would've been honest. It would've been bitter and inappropriate and the complete fucking opposite of fond sex but it would've been honest.

Kiss me.

Pause.

What are you afraid of? Honesty? It's just a kiss. I'm not going to bite your tongue off you coward.

Pause.

How can you tell me you love me when you won't even give me this?

Silence.

DAVID *moves towards* AMY.

He holds her and looks into her eyes.

He kisses her gently. Eventually she responds, more passionately than him. Her kiss becomes more desperate and forceful, she's clinging to him. He tries to end it, but she refuses to let him. She starts to cry. Eventually he ends the kiss and just holds her.

The End.

A Nick Hern Book

Unbroken first published in Great Britain as a paperback original in 2009 by Nick Hern Books Limited, 14 Larden Road, London W3 7ST, in association with the Gate Theatre, London

Unbroken copyright © 2009 Alexandra Wood

Alexandra Wood has asserted her right to be identified as the author of this work

Cover image: © Alberto Vajrabukka, www.flickr.com/vajra
Cover design: Ned Hoste, 2H

Typeset by Nick Hern Books, London
Printed and bound in Great Britain by CPI Antony Rowe, Chippenham, Wiltshire

A CIP catalogue record for this book is available from the British Library

ISBN   978 1 84842 021 2